The Sugar Factory

The Sugar Factory

■

Robert Carter

ATHENEUM ■ NEW YORK
1987

Copyright © 1986 by Robert Carter

Atheneum
Macmillan Publishing Company
866 Third Avenue, New York, N.Y. 10022
Collier Macmillan Canada, Inc.

Library of Congress Cataloging-in-Publication Data
Carter, Robert, 1945-
The sugar factory.
I. Title.
PR9619.3.C387S8   1987   823   87-12625
ISBN 0-689-11926-7

This is a work of fiction. Any references to historical events; to real
people, living or dead; or to real locales are intended only to give the
fiction a setting in historical reality. Other names, characters, and
incidents either are the product of the author's imagination or are used
fictitiously, and their resemblance, if any, to real-life counterparts is
entirely coincidental.

2 4 6 8 10 9 7 5 3 1

Printed in the United States of America

To my children,
Louise, Ben and Luke.

The Sugar Factory

1

This is the true story of things that happened to me not so long ago. Some of it is pretty disgusting and some of it you probably won't believe. The reason I'm telling it is because I sort of hope that every time someone reads it I'm going to feel a bit better; like someone helping to lift this great pole you're carrying, or something. Sounds a bit odd already doesn't it? I mean, how will I know whether anyone ever reads it or not?

Anyway, it starts when I'm waiting for the results of my exams. The last thing I remember hearing before sitting for them was, "They can shape and direct the rest of your lives." I mean, fancy telling you that before you sit for the bloody things. Some people have the sensitivity of a cheeseburger. Even though I am definitely your optimistic-type person, I figured then that if that shape-and-direction stuff was true, then "down" was likely to be my direction, and "blob" was likely to be my shape.

Actually the biggest puncture to my optimistic balloon came about five years before, when I found out I was supposed to be backward. The teacher told my mother, and even used the word "retarded". I heard her because I was standing under the window outside at the time. This teacher — Miss Imperago — showed my mother some of my books and said something like, "Look at these sentences, Mrs Berne. They're equivalent to a nine-year-old's, and Harris is thirteen." The school building must have just been painted because I can remember the smell of paint and the feel of concrete grooves in the wall making lines on my face. You can look pretty ridiculous with lines on your face from pressing up against things, so I don't do that anymore. Miss Imperago had these big tits. But that isn't what made me backward, even though I did used to think of them a lot. They were those very round sort, like a baby's bum. Nowadays I like smaller ones.

Anyway, my mum has a lot of respect for teachers, so she carried the news around like a kidney stone for a while, until she dropped it at the table one night. My dad actually went a bit strange about it. He was sitting at the table and his face went white. His lips went tight, in a straight line like a stretched rubber band.

"I don't want to hear that word," he said really soft, so you knew he meant it.

At the time, I wasn't too sure what "that word" was, but later I figured out he meant "retarded". Normally my mother ignored what he said when he was telling you what he didn't want. But not this time. She went off and cried in her bedroom, which was really pretty strange for her too.

We lived in this weatherboard house, then, where the timber slats slip into each other and run the same way as the ground. Underneath the house at one end there was enough space to just sit up. The wooden joists and bearers sat on little tin plates on top of these brick piers. When you first went under you couldn't see in the dark, you had to feel along the beams over your head and keep your fingers out of spider webs and splinters. In summer it was always like when you opened the fridge door, only without the light of course. I used to sit under there a lot, right from when I was very little, and make sugar. For a while there when I was little, my big brother used to help me make sugar, but he got tired of it. I never got tired of it. How you make sugar is, you get these rocks, sandstones they're called, and you hit them with something hard — a bricklayer's hammer is the best thing — and it all ends up like sugar. We used to wrap it up in newspaper in this special way so it sort of looked like bags of sugar. I would stack them up under the skinny end of the house, where you could only just crawl on your stomach and the cobwebs made you think there were spiders crawling in your hair. One day I think someone will find them and they will wonder who did it all.

After my father said he didn't want to hear "that word", I got under the house with a dictionary. You had to bring a torch if you wanted to read anything under there. I had this great torch, that had a flasher like a police light at one end. I swapped it for a photo album that my grandmother gave me, because I didn't have a camera anyway. The dictionary said:

> *Retard* (re-tard), v.t. to hinder progress; to make slow or late; to impede; with internal combustion engines, to time spark to take place late in engine cycle.

At the time, I found this a bit depressing. Dictionaries have never been much help to me. I think it is better not to know the meaning of some words. As a matter of fact I felt I had quite a good mind. Maybe not so good with things at school, but I knew it was there, perhaps like my sugar, waiting for someone to find it.

2

Underneath the house is where I first heard that Sharlene was going to live with us. You couldn't hear very well under the house unless you held this galvanised six-inch bolt up to your ear and put the other end on the floorboards. I think the sound carries down the bolt. Without it, the bolt I mean, you could just hear this muffled sound like the people above were all under water. Sometimes I did wonder if they buried you by mistake, I mean if you were still alive but couldn't move or anything, that it might be like being under the house. I used to think that I would have to take a galvanised bolt with me, just in case.

Getting back to Sharlene. Sharlene is my cousin. When she came to stay with us she was fifteen and I was fourteen. She had the small tits that I like now. She was also clever at school, but she couldn't ride a bike and she didn't like it under the house. I used to pretend I had to go to the toilet when she was in the bath, but she would never let me in. Sharlene had to live with us because her mother, my father's sister, ran away with another man. I used to picture Aunty Kathleen running away with this man, with them carrying all these suitcases, because Uncle George said they left him with nothing. It was impossible to imagine Aunty Kathleen running with anyone, she was so fat. It was the kind of fat you didn't mind though; like those negro singers. Like when she hugged you, you felt like looking to see afterwards if you'd made dents in her. I couldn't believe Aunty Kathleen had run away, I figured she had walked away. I wrote her a letter once, after she had left, because I thought she should come and see Sharlene. Sharlene must have missed her mother a lot because she used to cry in her room a fair bit, and I used to listen with my galvanised bolt. Aunty Kathleen never answered my letter and I realised later that I had sent it to her old address, the one she ran away from, which was very dumb. Sometimes I don't think enough about things.

When Sharlene arrived it was raining, and I had to get out of my bedroom and take all of my things with me to my brother's bedroom. Sharlene had to have her own room. I didn't mind too much, because, believe it or not, I used to get scared at night sometimes. My big brother, Lyndsay, didn't like the idea at all. He had his room arranged just how he liked it — sort of like the spare-parts showroom at the wreckers. He was nuts about cars and motorbikes and engines and stuff. All the little cracks in his fingers were black, filled up with sump oil and grease and car junk. He had to take three wheelbarrow loads of stuff to the shed, so I could fit into the room. He's very shy, but he can talk about mechanical stuff. He's not shy about that. He worked in a garage. He wasn't a qualified mechanic or anything, but everyone knew he could fix anything with oil in it and the owner of the garage paid him qualified mechanic's wages. Lyndsay always wanted his own garage, so he saved all his pay and hardly ever went out anywhere. I don't think Sharlene liked Lyndsay very much. She seemed to worry a lot about dirt and oil and grease, and whether it was going to get onto her or something. For some reason she always did seem to get a bit of it on her.

When she came in that day, all wet like next door's Irish setter, I said something really dumb like, "Geez you're wet."

"Yeah, but I'm going to dry out," she said, real sarcastic-like. She was a prickly little bastard at the beginning.

I said something like, "Titless wonder." And she punched me in the stomach. That was a bad time to get hit by Sharlene because I had just stopped being able to hit girls. There just never seemed any place that was proper to hit them. She was good looking though, with red hair — the good red — and perfect skin that you had to get your face right practically onto to see any spots. She smelled flawless too, like something you wanted to eat but weren't allowed to.

Sometimes she would watch me making something in the

old shed and she would stay and talk. The old shed was at the bottom of our yard, which was a long way from the house because we had this massive yard about four times the size of a normal block. My father built the shed before I was born. It's ridiculously strong and so bloody big you could fit six cars in it at once, even big ones. My dad always built things bigger and stronger than everyone else. I think because he always had big plans for everything. He was an "in case of" person. He carried a raincoat all the time, in case of rain; he took extra lunch with him, in case of hunger; he banked every spare piece of money, in case of emergency. Mum said it was the Depression that made him an "in case of" person, because he was proud and ate boiled wheat and spent nights in gaol, rather than ask for food. He used to talk about the Depression to us and I could never quite work it out, because while he was saying all about the misery and not getting a job and tramping around and everything, his eyes would be flashing as if he was remembering some dazzling dance or something. My father always looked more alive in the past than he ever did in the present.

I'll tell you more about my father later. The thing I want to tell you about now is my old high school at Chamberlain, and what happened there the day I first saw these things inside my head.

Chamberlain is this not-so-old, not-so-good state school about ten miles south of Sydney. Its only claim to fame was that one kid won the state high school javelin event eleven years before I got there. They still had the kid's picture in a glass case with the trophy, outside the principal's office. I used to imagine I could get my picture in the glass case and I practised throwing tomato stakes in our backyard until I put one through the windscreen of our neighbour's car. Most of the teachers at Chamberlain started hoping for a transfer about a week after they got there.

Anyway, on this Friday at Chamberlain we were having an English period, and it was as hot as hell. I got this unbelievable erection. It was the fast kind. The one that gets caught in your pants and sticks out like you've just opened an umbrella in there. While you're sitting down everything is okay, no-one can see anything, but if you have to stand up, my God. I had a couple of ways of handling this kind of erection. Method one was to put your hand in your pocket, grab it and make it go down your trouser leg (it didn't go down very far, mind you), but you had to be standing to be able to do that very satisfactorily. Method number two was to send it in the opposite direction, that is, towards your chin (it didn't go very far that way either) and you could hold it in place with your school case, if you were standing around with your schoolcase in your hand. This particular English period we had Mr Barker-White. I used to think it was Buggawhite at first, till I saw it written. He used to like the girls in the class better than the boys, which I didn't mind, because I did too. But he used to have these sort of jokes with the girls about the boys. Like for instance he'd ask some boy a question, like what is the symbolic meaning of such-and-such in so-and-so's novel? Of course the kid usually hadn't even read the book and he'd give some really dumb answer, and then old Barker-White would turn to the girls and say, "Now ladies, this is the kind of gentleman who will one day be asking you to step into his borrowed motor vehicle to whisk you away to a fantasy life in front of the drive-in theatre." Most of the girls would giggle their tits off at this, and the rest of us didn't know whether it was Barker-White or the girls we hated most.

On this particular Friday, I was sitting there with my fast erection, when Barker-White started looking for his next sacrifice. Sometimes in your life you get these feelings that start in your stomach and end up in the tips of your fingers and toes, that tell you "it's your turn", that you really can't escape it no matter what. I had that feeling when Barker-White looked at me that Friday. My erection turned to concrete.

"Berne, you look as though you've read our *Julius Caesar*." (Titters from the girls.) I sort of had read it, but with Shakespeare I could read it and get right to the end and I didn't know a thing about the whole bloody book.

"Was Brutus truly noble?" Barker-White was looking at

me with his eyebrows up and his head tilted back so I could see the inside bit of his nose which was all red and hairy. I knew Brutus stuck a knife in Caesar, but that was about it. What happened to me was, I just sort of froze up. My face got all hot and I thought the old erection was going to split my pants and knock the desk over. I said nothing. Barker-White stood up.

"Tell us what you know about Brutus," he said. What I knew about Brutus wasn't worth telling even if I could have told it.

"Stand up, boy," he said.

Now this was a real problem. In those days I was a very quiet person and I got embarrassed real easy. Like you only had to ask me to read a couple of lines of something out in class and I would just about shit myself. Well you can imagine how I would feel if I had to stand up with my pants all bulging out. So I couldn't stand up, could I?

"Did you hear me, Berne?" he said.

I put my hand in my pocket to see if I could give it a good old number one, down the leg. I think that was a mistake. I think Barker-White thought I was trying to act tough or something.

"Berne, what are you doing? Get your hand out of your pocket and stand up."

I figure people like this Barker-White must never have got any erections when they went to school. I mean if it had been a lady teacher, I could have understood. I mean, how would she ever know?

"Berne, do I have to come down there and drag you to your feet?"

No-one was laughing now, and Barker-White's face was getting all hunched up and his eyes were popping a bit. I wasn't going to stand up. He wasn't going to stop. Would you believe right at this time I got this unbelievable sort of really tired feeling, like I wanted to go to sleep. Everything was real still and hot and all slow-like. So here I am feeling like going to sleep. I figure when you get to the end of being scared you just get real tired.

"By God, Berne, you insolent little toad, I'll have you!"

Barker-White strode down the aisle between the desks, stopped in front of me and grabbed me by the collar. He had this scratchy check coat on that he always wore, hot or cold. The buttons on his sleeve scraped my face and pressed into my ear. He smelled like old flowers. I knew he was going to lift me to my feet. I was very light.

I think I sort of panicked when he started to lift me up by the collar. All I could think of was to hide my shame. What I did was, I put my arms under the desk so that as old Barker-White lifted me into the air, my whole desk came with me, as if it was glued to my front. It was very effective concealment, and took some strength on my part, but I would say that Barker-White was severely unimpressed. He couldn't manage to hold me up in the air as long as I could manage to hold onto the desk, so he let me and the desk drop. Now unfortunately Barker-White is one of these people who can't leave things unfinished. I mean he could have just had a big laugh with the rest of the class and said something witty like, "Berne has certainly grown attached to his work", and everyone would have felt he'd won and he was a big forgiver. But no, he's the kind of person who has to lose every damned pawn and piece on the board before he'll give up. Well, old Buggawhite still has lots of pieces on the board here with me, so he decides to bring in the headmaster, Mr Kingsley.

While he's coming, thanks be to God and biology, all the blood in my body has decided to run around my face, with the result that the old erection deflates and I return to normal. Barker-White stands over me and offers me up to the headmaster, who seems disappointed with my apparent normality. This was going to be difficult for Barker-White as I wasn't going to lift a desk again unless I had another erection to hide, and I reckoned I'd never have another one, either public or private, as long as I lived.

Anyway that tired feeling I told you about came back bigger than ever and I did this unbelievably great yawn. It was the kind where a little squirt of spit launches out, and would you believe it, it lands right on Barker-White's coat lapel.

9

Mercifully, old Kingsley drags me off to his office, I think to save my life more than anything else.

Old Kingsley gets me into his office and goes on about the school and discipline and learning and all that stuff that can really put you to sleep. Then he hits me with his cane, but not real hard, and tells me to sit outside his office on these long wooden benches. Actually that was a mistake. I was too tired to *sit* anywhere, so I went home. The problem with that was that you weren't supposed to go home in the middle of the day, especially if you had just lifted a desk and spat on a teacher. I did think about going to sleep on the benches but decided that might be worse than lifting and spitting, and going home.

I got home at 11.45 a.m. The house sounded empty. Sharlene had finished school some months before and she hadn't been able to get a job. I thought she would be out looking. My mother was shopping and my father was at work. One of my problems is that I'm not to be trusted on my own. What I mean is, you could trust me with secrets and stuff, and you could trust me if I was your friend, but you couldn't trust me not to look in your drawers and things if you went out, and you maybe couldn't trust me not to open your mail. I love mail. I enter competitions all the time just so I can get mail. Once I won a transistor radio with headphones, for picking out all the hidden things in this picture. But that's the only thing I've won. Actually the reason I keep entering competitions is because I like to think that all of the time there is a chance of something great happening, like I'll win something. And every time I don't win something I tell myself that makes it a bigger chance I will next time. That's statistics (my father says that's stupid).

Anyway, on this Friday, with no-one home, I got into Sharlene's room. I don't know why I went in there, probably to look through her drawers and things. Once I found this letter in Sharlene's drawer which must have been from a girlfriend of hers. This girlfriend was living in a squat in Darlinghurst. I didn't know what a squat was, but I didn't like the sound of it much. She kept saying in the letter that

Sharlene should join her and her friends because they were all having a good time. I didn't like the sound of this girlfriend and all her friends squatting around all over the place. Well, into Sharlene's room I go and there is Sharlene in bed with just a sheet over her, sort of like a corpse in a hospital show.

"What are you doing home?" she says.

Now apart from the shock of finding Sharlene there, I didn't really know why the hell I was home in the middle of the day. "I got tired," I said.

"What?"

"I got sick and they sent me home."

"Bullshit." Sharlene always seemed to know bullshit.

"I got into trouble."

"What for?"

"Not answering a question properly."

"Jesus."

"No, it was about Brutus."

"Don't be a smartarse."

"I squirted old Buggawhite, too."

"What with?"

"My spit."

"You spat on a teacher?"

"Well, sort of."

"You amaze me."

"It was sort of an accident."

"What happened after that?"

"The headmaster came and got me."

"Did he cane you?"

"Yes."

"Show me."

There were two faint red marks across my left hand. I felt like Charles Bronson. "It didn't hurt."

"You idiot. Why did you hold your hand out? They can't cane you if you don't hold your hand out."

"I don't know."

"So did they send you home?"

"No, I just walked off."

"Jesus."

"I felt really tired."

"You felt really tired."

"I just wanted to go to sleep."

"You're crazy."

"Mmmmmm."

"They'll get you when you go back tomorrow."

"Maybe I won't go back tomorrow."

"They'll make you, you're not fifteen yet."

"I could hide."

"Where would you hide?"

"I could piss off altogether."

"Where?"

"I could go to a squat."

"What?"

"In Darlinghurst, or somewhere."

"Have you been reading my mail?"

"Only one letter."

"I only got one letter."

"Well, that's probably the one I read."

"Jesus Christ."

Sharlene is just staring at me now, and I'm feeling as tired as hell. It is real quiet, except for the Beckhouse dog howling next door because he gets tied to the clothesline every day so he won't follow Mrs Beckhouse down the street. I tell Sharlene how I listen to people with my galvanised bolt. It's really hot. The air isn't moving and my nylon socks are itching my feet. I sit on the end of Sharlene's bed.

Inside my head I see a very small child
about five or six, carrying a tiny school case.
The pattern on her dress is blue and green checks.
I cannot see her face. She waves to me
from our front gate. I want to go with
her. I want her to come back. My
chest is hurting. It is as though I see
her at the end of a windy tunnel. The
tunnel is too narrow for me. Inside my
head I am frightened.

"Take your shoes off," she says.

I take my shoes and my socks off. The socks smell a bit. Sharlene holds the sheet up for me to get into bed alongside her. The Beckhouse dog has stopped barking. The side of my right arm just touches the side of her left arm. Her skin is cooler than mine. The house is surprisingly quieter than it is at night. At night the house shifts and creaks, and a cat or a bus or a siren cuts in all the time. I can feel Sharlene's cotton nightdress with the back of my hand, and I figure she hasn't even got up at all today. Her breathing is slow and deep; mine is fast and shallow. We just lie there breathing.

Going back to school the next day wasn't easy. Kingsley was waiting for me. I hoped it was curiosity, but it was revenge. I was to be an example. Every day for a week I was to be stood in front of the entire school at assembly time as an example, like being put in the stocks two hundred years ago. My only major problem was the fear of getting a fast erection, as an example to the whole school. Fortunately I didn't know then what I know now, about how fear can give you terrific erections.

When I wasn't being exposed to the school, Kingsley would have me in his office with one of my teachers for a sort of inquisition. The only teacher who had a bad word to say about me was old Barker-White. Most of the others said they virtually had never spoken to me. They looked unhappy. I think the trouble with some teachers is that they start off the year with too big hopes. The best teachers are the ones who aren't hoping too much.

3

I love Saturdays. When I was real little, about six or seven and Lyndsay was nine or ten, we used to sleep in this old saggy double bed that used to belong to my parents. Sometimes, on Saturday mornings when we woke up, Lyndsay would kiss me on the side of the face and I would kiss him. It was like when you kiss a baby because it gurgles at you. Lyndsay hated school then, much more than I did, and waking up on Saturday with the sun all crashing through the window with all the possibilities of a day for yourself was more than he could stand.

I remember one Saturday we decided to make some money from the neighbourhood kids. What we did was, we made up all these little stands and games, just like a school fête. We had hoop-la, and cans with sand in them to knock over, and lucky dips, and a chocolate wheel. We had prizes and things to buy, mostly from the local garbage dump, and our own odds and ends. We worked on it one entire Saturday from daybreak to dark, until our big yard was practically chock-a-block with flags and stalls and stuff. It was a smashing success. We must have had fifty kids busting their bums to spend their money the next day. I don't know how much we made, but Lyndsay bought six pigeons with his share and I don't remember what I did with mine. I still love Saturdays. Lots of people miss out on Saturdays because they're always getting ready for Sunday or Monday, or next year or something.

4

The person I fell in love with wasn't Sharlene; it was Mrs Helen McMillan. I called her Mrs Mac. Sometimes when I was fooling around I called her "Big Mac", like the hamburger. How I met Mrs Mac was through mowing lawns. I used to mow lawns for a few people after school and sometimes I would fix up their gardens. I really like the smell of cut grass. Some people say it's a sour smell, but I think it's more like sort of greenness and newness, if you know what I mean. I had this Victa petrol mower with a catcher that kept coming off unless I twisted a piece of wire around it, because the little bit of plastic that held it on was broken. One of the wheels was wobbly and I used to have a running contest between this wheel and me to see who won each row I mowed. If I won, then the row I cut was straight and clean; if the wheel won then the row had this curve or wriggle in it. Sometimes I let the wheel win just to keep things interesting.

I got paid four dollars for an average-sized lawn. Mrs Mac's lawn was bigger than average but I only charged her four dollars because she gave me a lime ice-cream soda half-way through the first time I cut her lawn. I figured she was fairly old because she had these two kids. One was about five and the other was just out of being a baby. I found out later that she had left her husband because he kept drinking all the time. I don't think he ever hit her or anything, but she was frightened for the kids, I reckon. The kids were called Julius, that's the five-year-old, and Clementine. I used to think they were really dumb names, but Helen, she liked them. But then she didn't have to wear them around. After a while I used to look forward to cutting her lawn. When she'd bring me the ice-cream soda, I used to turn the mower off and we'd sit on these old railway sleepers in the garden and talk.

Gardens are the best places to talk to people. The smells are better than house smells of deodorants and washing powder and fly spray. Mrs Mac told me about her family when she was little, and how she always wanted to own a bookshop, and what her first job was like. Sometimes I didn't understand what she was talking about, but I always used to enjoy listening to her. Which is pretty strange, really, because I always thought it was necessary to understand what was being said before you could enjoy it. She told me that most of the time we don't really understand what someone else is trying to say to us, but we don't have to understand to get the meaning. See what I mean, that's pretty hard to follow, isn't it?

How about this; once we were talking about love, and she said, "Love has no memory, we remember only ourselves loving — winning and losing, love has no use for memory." I think she was quoting some poet. I still don't know what it means, but I figure if I remember it so well, then it must be sort of "on hold" till I can understand it.

Sometimes Mrs Mac would ask me to babysit Julius and Clementine while she went shopping or something. Clementine was lovable, except she used to do these incredibly runny shits, and I could never get the nappy to go tight enough around her leg, so that when she stumbled and lurched around the place there would be this runny gravy down her leg and little brown spots over the floor; or worse still these little brown pellets I used to call "poo rolls". Julius was another matter. He hated me, and in the beginning I returned it with interest. Once he filled the petrol tank of my mower with salt, which took me four hours to clean out, and another time he gave Clementine a haircut when I was supposed to be minding them. Clementine had this thick black hair, like her mother's, which was amazing for a one-year-old. Old Julius was jealous because his must have been like his father's, sort of thin and colourless. I couldn't believe it when I saw what he'd done to Clementine's hair. I must have been watching something on television while he did it. I sometimes get absorbed in television, especially movies. Anyway, he'd cut her hair with scissors at first and then finished off with his mother's electric shaver. The result was mind-bending. Clementine had bits of her head showing through with these long black tufts and short greyish mown bits. She must have been frightened by the shaver, because when I saw her she had let go a couple of extra pounds of shit, and I nearly passed out. Helen didn't say much, she trimmed up Clementine's hair and locked up her shaver. I got little Julius back a week later. I heard him say he was going to be in the class play at school. He was going to be this giant carrot. Like all the kids in the class were going to be vegetables and do this dance and song about healthy food and nutrition and stuff. What I told him was that I had seen this play before and what really happened was that all the rotten kids got carrot parts because at the end of the play they got put into this giant blender, and puréed. Julius got sick for a week and wouldn't go to school until the play was over.

I was sitting in the garden after finishing Helen's lawn, not long after Julius's sick week, when she sat down and asked me where I was going.

"Nowhere, I'm just waiting to cool off," I said.

"I mean *in life*, Harris, where are you going in life?"

"Oh, there," I said, real dumb-like.

"Yeah, there."

"Nowhere, I'm just waiting to warm up." Sometimes I can say things that make people laugh, but I can never seem to say them when I want to, they always come out when *they* want to. Helen laughed. She ruffled my hair like she thought I was real cute or something.

"And when you warm up ... ?"

"I don't know."

"What about the Police Force?"

It so happened old Frank, that's the husband she left, was a policeman. "I don't think so. I haven't got a big enough chest. You have to have a muscly chest, the careers teacher at school told me."

"What about teaching?"

"Not enough brains."

"What about building, like your father?"

"Too much brains."

She laughed. "There must be something you're interested in."

"Yeah, I'd like to work in a forest." Now don't tell me where that idea came from, I swear I'd never thought of it in my life. But there it was.

"Doing what?"

"I don't know. Maybe I could work in parks and places."

Helen is the type of person who you end up saying stuff to that you haven't ever really thought about, and afterwards you start thinking about what you said, and all you can do is shake your head and smile at what you've done. But you never go back to the place you were at before you said the stuff you said.

"You could be a Ranger," she said.

"A Ranger?"

"A Forest Ranger; you know, they drive around in four-wheel drives and look after wildlife sanctuaries and protect plants and animals."

"That sounds all right — what do you have to do to be one?"

"I'm not sure, but I'll bet you could do it."

I felt like ruffling her hair for saying that, but I'm not the kind of person who ruffles people's hair. I just slurped on the dregs of my ice-cream soda.

Have you ever noticed how the good things always seem to have happened in the past? I look back sometimes and I think, "Why didn't I love it more at the time? You know, wallow and splash around in it, like a duck in a puddle." And then I realise I'm doing the same thing right at the moment, that one day I'll say about right now, this moment, "Why didn't I love it more?"

"You could be a Forest Ranger, Harris. I'll bet you could."

"You just want to drive around in my four-wheel drive."

"Of course. Come on, I'll ring up Parks and Wildlife or

someone, and we'll find out what you have to do."

I watched her ring about five thousand different numbers and hold on forty million times until she got what she wanted to know.

"You have to pass their entrance exam."

"I thought so."

"No, but it's very easy, so the lady said."

"It'd have to be."

"You could do it, Harris."

"Maybe."

"I'll help you."

That afternoon I told her not to pay me for the lawn because of all the phone calls, but she said that good old Frank sends her a cheque every month and she gets a deserted wife's pension, even though it was her who did the deserting. A week later she had all the information, past exam papers and stuff about Forest Rangers.

Well, that's how come I happen to be waiting for the results of my exams. They have this entrance exam, the Parks and Wildlife Service, that if you pass, then you can get an interview to see if you can be a Ranger.

5

For three afternoons a week, Mrs Mac would help me with studying for the Ranger's exams. She is what I would call a natural teacher. Anyone who could teach me with rotten Julius and smelly Clementine around would have to be real talented. Anyway, whole scads of stuff I didn't know started falling into place like Lego blocks snapping together, and even my thinking started improving. At the end of one session, she put her arm around my neck and kissed me on the forehead and said, "You're really nice, Harris."

Up until then I'd never really thought of myself as nice. I mean we were just finishing factorising these equations and I couldn't see how I'd been very nice. I thought I'd been a bit shitty, actually. You know, like pretending that the reason I was having trouble with it was because she wasn't explaining it properly, rather than the fact that I couldn't understand it. I really felt like kissing her forehead back, but I didn't. There's lots of things I don't do that I want to do with people.

After that kiss, I used to have these sort of dreams when I was awake. Mrs Mac would kiss my forehead, and then I would kiss hers and then she would kiss my face and I would kiss hers, and so on. And then we would be kissing each other all over, until I was puffing and my mouth was all wet and I just sort of shut my mind down. I could bring it all back whenever I wanted to, but I had to be a bit careful because I must have been doing it when mum was talking to me once, because she hit me on the back of the head and asked me whether I was in gaga land.

Mrs Mac taught me to play chess. She said chess is a discipline of the mind and the emotions. Well, nobody needed a bit of discipline of the mind and emotions more than me, but I don't think that was why she taught me. She just didn't have anybody to play with. After we finished studying, she would get out the chessboard and away we would go. I could never beat her, even though I got pretty good because I used to practise at home under the house with a little magnetic set. She was always chuckling away when she played chess, and frankly it used to give me the shits, but I don't think she knew that. I like people to be real quiet when they play chess. That way you can at least think you've got them worried a bit, even if you lose.

6

Well, there I was, like I said, waiting for the results of my exams. I could see the postman coming. I knew he had my exam results in there. My hands had gone all sweaty and I could feel that vein in my neck ticking away. My stomach was getting these little electric spirals. He handed a bunch of letters to me. I knew mine was the brown one that was longer than the others. I was a bit shocked at how I felt so frightened about this letter. This was the first time I had been frightened by a letter. There were three sections to the exams and you had to pass all three. I held the brown envelope up to the sun, but I couldn't see through it. My hands were shaking. I went inside the house and put the other letters on the dining-room table. I squashed the brown envelope between my finger and thumb to feel how thick the letter inside was. I guessed that it was only one sheet thick. I thought about how this letter might change the direction and shape of my life, like the man said. I didn't realise before how much I wanted to pass this exam.

It was Tuesday morning, the second week of the school holidays. I had to mow Mrs Mac's lawn. Mrs Mac would be home, washing or cooking something, or working in the garden. She could open it for me. I took the mower and pushed it at break-neck speed in front of me to Mrs Mac's.

She was in the bath when I arrived with the brown envelope. I yelled through the door. "The exam results are here."

"Jesus Christ, Harris, you scared me."

"I'm sorry."

"Well, tell me, what the hell did you get?"

"I haven't opened it yet."

"What?"

"I thought you could open it, you might be luckier than me."

"I'll be out in a minute."

She came out with this old flannelette dressing-gown on. She was all red and wet and steamy looking. I followed her into the kitchen while she took down two glasses and poured a small amount of brandy or something into each one. She topped mine up with coke and handed it to me.

"Whichever way it goes we'll need this, and some music."

She turned the radio onto 2UW which was playing four-in-a-row, and sat down.

"Here." I passed her the envelope.

"Maybe we should leave it for a few days," she teased.

"Bullshit," I said eloquently.

She slid her finger under the flap and split the edge of the envelope. There was only one sheet, neatly folded twice. 2UW was playing an old David Bowie song about this astronaut who couldn't get back from outer space.

My drink was gone and I hadn't even tasted it. Helen was reading the result form. I couldn't tell from her face whether it was good or bad.

"You sure you don't want to be a Policeman?" she asked.

"Tell me what it says."

"It says, Harris Berne, candidate 0017; results of examination for Entrance Traineeship Ranger, Department of Parks and Wildlife. Section A — Pass; Section B — Pass; Section C — Pass."

"God, shit, I passed."

"You did, Harris, you did."

I had this really stupid grin stuck on my face, and Helen had funny eyes, like laughing ones. 2UW had moved on to Willie Nelson.

"It says here you have an interview on Monday, eighteenth April."

"When is the eighteenth?"

"About six weeks."

"What time?"

"Ten thirty."

"Bloody hell, I passed."

"Now I can ride in your four-wheel drive."

"I don't think they give you one at the interview. I may not even pass the interview."

"You will, you will. That's only a formality."

Willie Nelson was probably wiping sweat off his face or something with that dirty thing he wears around his neck, because the singing had stopped and there was only this scrawny guitar playing. I remember that, and the taste of the brandy in my mouth as I went over to Helen and kissed her on the lips. It was supposed to be a "thank you, I like you very much" kiss, but it turned out to be a "thank you, I love you" kind of kiss.

Good timing has never been one of my strong points. And this was no exception, because there was a knock at the door. Who should be standing at the door, but old Frank, Mrs Mac's Mr Mac. I could hardly believe it when she brought him in and introduced me. He didn't look anything like I imagined. He was tall, with a big chest, and pale looking, not big and fat with a beard. Mrs Mac hadn't seen Frank since she moved away, so everything seemed a bit tense. He kept apologising all the time and saying he didn't mean to interrupt or anything. I kept wiping my mouth as if Helen's lips and half her face were still stuck on there or something. Shit, I felt uncomfortable. Helen told him about my exam results, and he shook my hand, real polite-like. Instead of this making me feel all equal, I felt like I shrank and I should have been outside playing with old Julius.

Fortunately, I can always lie when I need to, so I said I had this extra big lawn to mow away on the other side of town, so I had to go, but it was nice to meet you and all that crap. All of it was a lie, especially the part about being nice to meet him. I wished he was back in a gutter or a park or wherever drunks go. I wished *he* was seventeen, and I was her husband. I wished Helen and I were driving off in a four-wheel drive somewhere, even if bloody Julius and Clementine were rolling around in the back.

On the way home from Mrs Mac's, I'm pushing the mower and I run into this kid called Kyle; Bruce Kyle. He's the sort of kid you know would make a really great bouncer or an experimenter on animals. He was famous at school because he squashed this frog in his bare hands, while he was eating an onion sandwich, would you believe. He had this body like on a statue I saw at the National Gallery once when the school went there on an excursion. Everyone was a bit scared of Kyle. I don't think Kyle actually *liked* squashing the frog, but then I don't think he minded either. I make sure the mower is between us.

"Where are you going?" he says to me.

"Just home," I answer, real polite, like he's my favourite person in the world.

"Where've you been?"

"Up at Mrs Mac's — Mrs McMillan's. I mow her lawn." I'm smiling now as if mowing lawns is just right for little shits like me.

"How much do you get?"

"Four dollars."

"That's not much."

"I don't do much of a job." I hate myself.

"Is she the one who got left by her husband?"

"I think she left him, actually."

"She must be dying for it."

"Yeah, probably," I say. I have this picture of me in court explaining how the lawn mower started up by itself, because it was overheated, and then went straight over poor Bruce's face.

"Are you giving it to her?"

"Me?" I ask, like as if I haven't even got one or something.

Kyle looks at me as if I am a frog, or maybe an onion sandwich.

"What does she do for you?"

"She brings me a lime ice-cream soda."

"What about cutting the grass in her bedroom."

"Ha ha ha." I happen to have this really shithouse laughter. I used to practise laughing under the house, trying to

25

get it right. But I never did. My mother was watering the camellias near the house once when I was practising and she threatened to have me locked up. So I gave it up. Laughing makes me very tense. Like if someone is telling me a joke, especially a real long one, then I start getting ready to laugh about half-way through because I can't stand it if no-one laughs at someone's joke. Even Kyle can tell a phoney laugh.

"Maybe I could come along with you next time?"

"Ha ha ha."

"You could do the lawn while I do her."

"Ha ha ha." Laughing does save you from talking, though.

Kyle comes around the lawn mower and stands practically on my sneakers. He wears these really opened-up shirts, and I can see hair starting to grow on his chest. I figure he's getting more there than I'm getting on my face, maybe my whole body. "Listen, how about a loan?" he says, like I was his little brother.

"I'm sorry, Bruce, but I haven't got any money at the moment," I say, while I start this big search in my pockets as if I might have forgotten a few thousand somewhere.

"Come on, you're just coming back from mowing her lawn."

"She didn't pay me today. Someone came, a visitor, and she forgot to pay me."

"You're a prick." He says this like someone would say, "Pass me the salt!" His face doesn't change.

"Ha ha ha," I say.

"You're a prick," he says again.

"I've got to go now Bruce, I'll see ya."

"You're a stupid prick."

"Ha ha ha," I say.

"Go back and get it now," he says with his nostrils breathing all over my face.

"Get what, Bruce?" I ask patiently.

"The money for the lawn, stupid."

"I can't. She's got this visitor."

"So what, she might give you a tip if she's got a visitor."

"I can't do that, Bruce, see my father wants the mower home right now." Quick lies are never my best ones.

"I'll go back then, and I'll tell her you sent me for the money," he says.

I know he has to be bluffing. I say, "Ha ha ha," like he's a big joker.

"Let's both go then," he says.

"I can't Bruce, because my German Shepherd meets me along the way home, not too far from here actually, and he gets very upset if I'm late."

"How far is it to her place?" he says. I don't think Kyle is even afraid of German Shepherds.

"It's a fair way."

"Well, let's go, I wouldn't want you to be late home. Your German Shepherd's got to mow the lawn."

"Ha ha ha," I say, but I keep seeing that frog.

"Leave the mower here," he says.

"Shit, Bruce, I can't do that, someone might take it. Look, you wait here with the mower and I'll run back to Mrs McMillan's and get the money."

"Okay," he says.

"I won't be long," I say as I jog off. I think about never coming back. A new identity in South America. I could work in a copper mine and breed llamas.

I hope Frank is not there when I get to Helen's. At the front gate is Julius; he is bouncing a tennis ball on the pathway, trying to kill a little black ant with each hit.

"What do you want?" Julius says.

"Where's your mother?" I ask.

"Dunno."

"Is ... is ... ," I realised I didn't know what to call Frank to Julius. "Is there anyone with her?"

"My dad," he says.

"What room are they in?"

"I dunno," he says.

I go around to the back of the house. The grass smells good. I was hoping they would be in the garden, but they are not. I go to the back door and knock. There is no answer. I knock again, louder. There is no answer. I think of Bruce Kyle standing with my lawn mower and smoking Chesterfields. I open the back door and go inside. I can hear Clementine, and practically smell her too. She must have just woken up and begun googling in her cot. I get this picture of Helen and Frank wrestling on the floor with no clothes on. I am shaking again, like when I got the brown envelope. I am surprised that this time I am also angry.

"Harris, what are you doing here?" Helen says. She is still wearing the cotton dressing-gown, and she is truly surprised to see me as she comes out of the bathroom.

"I forgot something," I said.

"What did you forget?"

I saw the brown envelope on the table. "My exam results," I said.

"Did you see Julius outside as you came in?"

"Yes, he's killing ants on the front path."

"Harris, I'm very pleased you passed."

"So am I."

"I think you will be okay at the interivew. Just be yourself. If they don't like that, then you're better off not working for them."

Helen has this way of making things you're afraid of seem really insignificant. I thought of telling her about Kyle, but decided against it. "It was nice to meet Frank," I said.

"Frank's very nice."

"He seemed very nice."

"Not being nice isn't Frank's problem."

I must have looked towards the bedroom or something because she said, "He's not here, he's gone."

"Julius said he was still here."

"You know Julius."

"Is he coming back?"

"Probably to see the children from time to time."

"It's tough luck about the drinking."

"The drinking is not Frank's problem, it's the result of his problems. Frank expects too much of himself and of everything else."

"Like a perfectionist."

"Yes, in a way."

"There was this kid in our class last year, he was a perfectionist. He used to always count up the things he got wrong. Like as if that was more important than the stuff he got right. He used to get most of it right though."

"Would you like a drink, Harris?"

"No, I've got someone waiting for me."

"Oh, a girlfriend?"

"No, it's just a kid from school."

"Well, good luck with the interview."

"Yeh, well, thanks for helping and everything."

"That's what friends are for."

"I'll see ya, Helen."

"See you, Harris."

When I left Helen, I felt a bit strange, sort of a bit like crying and laughing and wanting to be on my own. I get like that sometimes, like when I walk along beaches when it's nearly dark, and too cold to swim. On the way out the front gate, I took the tennis ball off Julius and threw it into the next-door neighbour's garden. I did it half for little shit Julius, and half for the little black ants.

Unfortunately, the closer I got to the mower and Kyle, the less I felt like being on a beach and the more I felt like being in South America. It wasn't until I was practically up to him that I realised I didn't get the money.

"Did you get the money?" he says.

"No, they must have gone out."

"What the bloody hell took you so long then?" Kyle comes over to me and grabs the front of my shirt. One of the buttons pops off. He feels the envelope in my shirt pocket. "What's this?" he says.

"It's nothing, just a letter."

He rips the envelope out of my pocket. In his hands it definitely looks like a frog. He takes out the letter, unfolds it and starts to read it.

"Harris Berne . . . results of . . . Traineeship Ranger . . . "

"Ha ha ha," I say.

"What are you going to be — the Lone Ranger?" he says.

"Ha ha ha," I say.

"They gonna give you a horse and cowboy hat too," he starts laughing and it sounds like, "Haair haair haair haair."

I think about hitting him and running, but then I remember the lawn mower, and I reckon he'd take it to pieces the permanent way.

"Ha ha ha," I say.

"Hey you've got yourself an appointment here, Berne. They probably want you to mow their lawns, haair haair haair."

"Ha ha ha, well I have to get going now, Bruce," I say very politely. I hold my hand out for the letter. He ignores my hand.

"Listen," he says, a bit pally like, "start the mower up for us."

"What for?" I ask.

"I wanta see it go," he says.

"There's not much petrol left."

He takes the top off the petrol tank. "There's enough."

"Okay." I turn the petrol on, and pull on the starting cord. It doesn't start right away. It never does start right away. It coughs and blows blue smoke a few times, then it splutters into life.

Kyle throws my letter and the envelope to the ground in front of the mower. "Try it out on that," he says.

"I can't cut that up, Bruce, that's my exam results and my appointment."

"Run over it, you little prick," he says.

I push the mower forward towards the letter and chop it up very efficiently, along with the back half of Kyle's shoe and a piece of his foot. It must have been the wheel that did it, or God, or something, because I never would have been game enough by myself.

Kyle's foot stopped the mower dead, and his scream just about stopped the traffic. The first thing I looked for was whether he was mobile or not. He wasn't. He was clutching his heel and there was blood everywhere. You might think that this was very satisfying. It wasn't. I had visions of a one-legged Kyle hunting me down in Bolivia.

"Jesus Christ, Bruce, are you all right?"

"Aaaaaaaaaaaaaaaaaaaaggggggghhhhhhhhhh," he said.

"Stay there. I'll get an ambulance."

A lady from across the road called out, "Do you want me to ring for an ambulance?"

"Yes," I said. I knew you were supposed to stop the bleeding but I couldn't bring myself to get too close to him. "Hold your hand on it, Bruce, to stop the bleeding," I said.

"Aaaaaaaaaaaaaaaaaaaaggggggghhhhhhhhhh," he said.

"It was the wheel, Bruce. This back wheel is completely unpredictable. I've wiped out more flowers and cats' tails. I have to get it fixed, before I chop someone's foot off."

"Aaaaaaaaaaaaaaaaaaaaaaaaggggggggggggghhhhhhhh," he said.

I looked around for a part of his foot that might have to be sewn back on, but there wasn't any. I knew you are supposed to keep it in ice water or something.

Thank God the ambulance came quickly and took him away. I find it hard to deal with people who can't take pain very well.

I wasn't too worried about chopping up my letter. I knew the interview was April eighteenth, at ten thirty. I was worried about Bruce Kyle, though, and I decided to send him a get well card and maybe an early Christmas card as well, with four dollars in it.

Sharlene and Lyndsay and my mother were sitting in the kitchen talking when I got home. I decided not to tell them about Kyle's foot.

"I passed the exams," I said.

"Did you dear, that's wonderful," my mother said.

"Good on ya, Hassa!" Lyndsay said. Lyndsay always called me Hassa.

"So you're going to be a Forest Ranger. God help the gum trees," Sharlene said.

"When do you start? my mother asked.

"I haven't got the job yet. I've got an interview in April."

"Lyndsay's got some good news too," my mother announced.

"I'm getting married," Lyndsay said.

Lyndsay looked all embarrassed. We had hardly talked about his girlfriend, Jacquiline, at all. Everything about Jacquiline was short; her hair, her legs, her conversation, and her memory. She never remembers I hate being called Harry. She is even a short reader. She reads only magazines — *House and Garden*, *Home Beautiful*, and *Cooking for Thrifties* or something.

My reaction, as is often the case, was pretty inadequate. "What for?" I asked.

Sharlene, as was often the case, rescued me. "Because that's what people do when they grow up, dummy."

"When is it?" I asked.

"The end of next month. You can't be best man. Jacquiline's brother wants to be, and she promised him."

Lyndsay looked really uncomfortable.

"That's okay," I said to him. "I hate those things where everyone expects you to do all that stuff."

"Well I'd rather have you," Lyndsay said. "But Jacquiline has sort of promised him."

"Where are you going to live?" I asked.

"They've rented a nice little place at Greening Hills," mother said.

Greening Hills is like this house graveyard. You know what those European World War II cemeteries look like with those millions of little white crosses, all perfectly lined up ... well that's Greening Hills, only they're houses. I mow a lawn down there for Mrs Wang Htsu, or something. I call her Mrs Soo. She's from Vietnam and she has really great manners. She's always smiling and paying me too much money. Mrs Soo does seem real happy down there but I think she is just happy to be anywhere. I thought about Lyndsay living down there and it made me feel depressed.

"It's a nice place," Lyndsay said. "Jacquiline found it.

We might be able to buy it after a year or two."

"We should have a celebration," Sharlene said.

"I'll make some tea." My mother always celebrated by making tea.

7

The Saturday morning before the Monday of my interview, Mrs Mac asked me to mind Julius and Clementine while she went shopping. I think she liked to get by herself sometimes, away from the children, more than she wanted to do any real shopping. I didn't mind too much. She always brought back these fresh bread rolls and we would have them with peanut butter and honey. She would talk about a dress she saw in a window or how the bus driver flirted with her. She sometimes seemed a lot younger when she came back from shopping, and I could tell what kind of a kid she had been. She would have been the kind of kid that everyone likes, you know always getting excited about things and knowing everybody's birthday, with the kind of hair that's "fly-away" curly.

Julius was mostly a pain when his mother was around, but Clementine always grabbed hold of my leg and hugged it every time I came. Clementine wasn't much of a talker. She used to call me Hazz and she would sit on my lap and make me do "round and round the garden" on her toes about a million times, and every time she would giggle her head off. She had this book called *A Pipe Dream*, which had fantastic drawings and you had to find all these hidden people and things in it. When I wouldn't play "round the garden" any more, she would haul out her raggedy old book and we would pretend to find all the hidden things as if we had never seen them before. The funny thing is, I never got tired of doing it. I used to sometimes think of her father and how he must especially miss Clementine and doing things like that with her.

With his mother away, Julius liked to play hide-and-seek through the house and poor old Clementine could never quite figure it out. She used to follow me around trying to get me to chase her. She would give this high-pitched squeal when I did chase her, and she would giggle and lurch off in her idea of running, and half the time she would shit herself. I never could believe how a little kid could produce so much shit — all the time, I mean. I told Helen we called the game hide-and-shit.

We were playing hide-and-shit this Saturday morning. Julius was getting very cunning at finding places to hide and he made me count to five hundred before I came looking for him. This time he had taken Clementine with him. I checked all the regular places Julius used to hide; in the wardrobes, the kitchen cupboards, under the beds, in the jacaranda tree, and the garden shed, but no Julius or Clementine. After a while I began to get a bit worried. I called out for Julius. "I give up, Julius, I give up, you can come out now. Clementiiiiiiiiine, Clementiiiiiiine." I used to sing this song, "Oh my darling, Oh my darling, Oh my darling, Clementine" and Clementine would always come running at me squealing to be picked up. I sang the first verse and the chorus of the song, but she didn't appear.

I checked all the rooms again, more thoroughly, then I heard a truck horn blowing in the street outside. My muscles went all rubbery and I couldn't get the front door open because it used to catch on the carpet because one of the hinges was broken. I ran to the back door, flung it open and raced into the street. The truck was stopped on the other side of the road. It was a Kenworth with a large aluminium trailer that carries coal or gravel. I couldn't see the driver. The motor of the truck was a diesel that wobbled the truck and spewed thin black smoke out of this chrome exhaust pipe. The truck just sat there, chack chack chacking away. I looked for Julius and Clementine. I could see the driver's head showing over the bonnet in front of the truck. I ran over to him.

"Bloody thing's been rattling all morning," he said.

"You didn't see two little kids out here?" I asked him.

"Nope, I just came from Lithgow," he said.

"Thanks."

"Are you all right?"

"Yes thanks," I said. "I'll see ya."

Coming back into the house, I was getting a bit angry. I started yelling out for them both to come out or I would kill them slowly and painfully. That didn't work, and neither did a promise of two Mars bars each. I tried, "Here comes your mother with some presents," and, "Look at this little kitten I just found," but that didn't work either. I turned the television on and tried to sit them out for ten minutes, but neither of them appeared. I started another search of the house. In Helen's bedroom there was a pile of clean washing heaped on the bed. Julius was under the washing. I could hear his breathing as he slept.

"Julius, you little bastard, didn't you hear me calling you?" I yelled at him. "You've got mud all over your mother's washing." Julius got to his feet all groggy-looking from sleep.

"Mummy," he said.

"Where's Clementine?"

"I want mummy."

"Tell me where Clementine is."

"Don't know."

"Did you hide her?"

"Is mummy home?"

"No, she isn't. Listen, Julius, would you please tell me where Clementine is. I'll have to change her."

"No."

"Look, Julius, she's only a little baby. She might be lost or something."

"You have to find her."

"You did hide her then?"

"You have to find her by yourself."

"I can't find her, Julius, for Christ's sake."

"You have to find her, 'cause you're 'in'. "

"I know I'm 'in', but I can't find her, you little moron."

"She's in the house."

"She's not in the bloody house. I'd have heard her if she was."

"You have to find her yourself."

"Jesus, shit. What room is she in then? Give me a clue."

"I'm not telling you till mummy comes home."

"Julius I'm going to twist your arm around, see, like this ... "

"Owwww, don't."

"Until you tell me where she is."

"Owwwwwwwwwwwww."

"Your arm will come off if I keep going."

"Owwwwww, she's in the kitchen."

"She's not in the kitchen, Julius, I've looked."

"Owwwwwwwwwwwwwwwwwwwwwww."

"Where, Julius?"

"In the 'frigerator."

"What?"

"In the 'frigerator."

"Jesus, Julius, did you put her in ... "

Coming into the kitchen, I got this big feeling of wanting to go to the toilet. I was hoping that Julius was trying to trick me, that he hadn't really put Clementine in the refrigerator.

I pulled open the door. What Julius had done, while I was counting to five hundred, was, he had stacked all the things in the refrigerator up the top, and sat Clementine in the bottom.

Inside my head there was the tiny five-year-old again, with her school bag and her blue and green uniform.
I could not see her face. Someone was holding her hand. She was trying to wave to me. My fingers were poking through the chain wire of our gate. She was walking away and looking back to me over her shoulder.
Inside my head.

Clementine was all scrunched up, and her face was this colour like I'd never seen on anything before. She wasn't moving, her eyes were shut and she had shit all over her. I pulled her out by her legs and they felt very cold. I held on to her very tightly to try and warm her up. Hot water was the only thing I could think of so I filled the sink with warm water and sat her in it. I think I must have been frightened she wasn't breathing because I never looked close enough at her to see whether she was. She wasn't crying or making any noises, and I noticed that. The water in the sink was all brown and the smell was making me feel sick.

Helen came through the kitchen door right at that moment and she screamed this really horrible scream, sort of like an animal, when she saw us. And that's all that I remember happening for a while.

I stayed till the ambulance took Clementine and Helen and Julius away. Helen kept asking me what happened in this high-pitched voice, but she never listened for me to answer. I cleaned up the sink and the refrigerator. There was nothing else to do, so I went home.

I think that's when I started dealing with God. I offered God this deal. That if Clementine didn't die, then I would give up trying to be a Ranger and live in Greening Hills, and I would give half of my lawn-mowing money to the orphans or something. When you think about it, except for the money, God wasn't getting much of a deal. I just thought that the more I could suffer, the better God would like it. I don't offer that kind of bargain anymore.

8

Lyndsay and Jacquiline were sitting around the table in the kitchen with my mother and father. The only big part of Jacquiline was in full swing, showing her fifty-or-so virginal white teeth. I wasn't thinking of Clementine or Mrs Mac or anything, I just felt sort of sleepy. "Sit down, Harry," she says, "We're talking about the wedding."

"Where's Sharlene?" I ask.

"Shopping," my mother says. "Jacquiline thought you might like to say something at the wedding."

"A speech?"

"Sort of, like responding on behalf of the bridesmaids." Jacquiline aims all her teeth at me.

"No, I don't want to do that."

"Well we can work all that out later," Jacquiline smiles. "Do you think we should have a band, Harry?" she says.

"Well that would be a change from the old organ."

"Not in the church, silly, at the reception."

"He's just being smart," my dad says.

"What sort of band?" I asked.

"What type do you think, Harry?"

I couldn't help feeling sorry for Jacquiline; trying to win me over was a bit like trying to feed a cranky old dog.

"What about a punk band?"

"He's just being his usual smart-arse self," says my dad to my mother.

"We wouldn't be able to dance to that," says Jacquiline.

"What about a dance band?"

"Brilliant," says Lyndsay.

"Could you find one perhaps, Harry?" Jacquiline never gives up.

"Don't leave it to him. You'll end up with one of those

Raggo bands with everyone hitting tin cans with six-inch nails," my dad says to Lyndsay.

"Reggae," says Lyndsay.

"I think Harris could find a proper band, couldn't you dear?" says my mum.

"How much do you want to spend?"

"Very little," my dad says to my mum. He was paying because Jacquiline's father had died ten years ago and her mother didn't earn much. She worked at the Pizza Hut, mostly on the ovens but sometimes on the tables. She used to give me a free Pepsi when she could get away with it. I liked her better than Jacquiline. I couldn't see Jacquiline risking free Pepsis for anyone.

I was feeling okay, really, I wasn't thinking of Clementine or anything, when Sharlene burst in.

"Do you know what just happened?" Sharlene says.

"What?" says my father to my mother.

"Mrs McMillan, you know the lady Harris mows the lawn for, her baby has just been rushed to hospital."

"You were just down there, Harris?" My mother looks at me as if for an explanation.

"I don't know anything," I lied. I don't think anyone in the family, even Lyndsay, knew much about anything I did, which wasn't their fault. It always seemed a bit embarrassing when I tried to tell someone, and anyway they always seemed like they were having enough problems of their own without adding any of mine. I don't think they knew how I felt about Mrs Mac, or how I minded her kids and things like that.

"What was wrong with the baby?" my mum asked Sharlene.

"Nobody knows. They just saw the ambulance and it had its siren on," Sharlene said.

"Never should have left her husband," my father said.

"He was an alcoholic, dear," my mother said.

"Even so."

"I do believe he comes back at night occasionally," my mother says. Underneath, I don't think my mother likes women. "She probably went out and left it on its own."

"She has a five-year-old boy as well," Sharlene says.

"Well, that's what has happened," says my mother. "She's gone out and left the five-year-old to mind the baby. People like that don't deserve to have children."

Inside my head I waited at our gate for the blue and green checked girl.

"I never left mine when they were little," says my mother.

"I wouldn't have stood for it," says my father.

"It wouldn't have had anything to do with you."

"Wouldn't it, by Christ?"

"You had nothing to do with them when they were little."

"I used to bath and feed them."

"Once a week."

"I wonder if we should do anything?" says Sharlene.

"Well there's not much we could do, is there?" my mother says.

"Best off to stay out of people's business," says my father.

"She must have relatives."

"Might send her back to her husband."

"Sharlene, Harry is going to get the band for our wedding," says Jacquiline.

"My mother went off and left me. I suppose she didn't deserve to have children either," says Sharlene.

"That was different, dear. You weren't little and helpless," says my mother.

"Bloody hell, do we have to talk about all this?" says Lyndsay.

"Can we get back to the guest list?" smiles Jacquiline.

I left the kitchen, walked through the garden, around to the side of the house, and then underneath to the sugar factory. I thought about ringing the hospital, but I just sat there. I wondered what Mrs Mac would be doing, what she would be thinking. The old rusty brick-layer's hammer was still there. I began pounding on some sandstone. It was a long

41

time since I had done this but the rhythm was as familiar as breathing.

I must have been crushing away for about an hour when the dark shape of a body crouched against the light at the side of the house.

"Are you under there, Harris? I can't see."

It was Sharlene. She crawled under the house and moved close to me. I stopped hammering.

"Did you like that Mrs McMillan and her baby?"

"Yes."

"I'm sorry, Harris." I began pounding at the rock again.

"Will we talk about it?" she asked.

"No," I said.

Sharlene waited a long time without saying anything while I smashed up the sandstone.

"Is this the galvanised bolt?" she asked, as she held it up to me.

"Yes, that's it," I said.

"What do I do with it, again?"

"Hold it up onto the floorboards, and put your ear to the other end."

"Christ, it really works."

"I know."

"I can hear them up there now. Shit, your mother's arguing with Jacquiline about the colours of something or other. Probably Lyndsay's eyes are going to clash with the cake."

"He'll have to keep them shut then."

"Or she'll have them tinted."

"Or make him wear glasses."

"Or have them replaced."

"She's really not that bad," I said.

"I know," Sharlene said. She waited quietly again.

"Harris."

"What?"

"Do you sometimes hear things you're not meant to hear?"

"Sometimes."

"Why do you do it, then?"

"I don't know."

"Maybe you're a voyeur."

"Maybe."

"Do you know what that is?"

"No."

"It's someone who only gets pleasure out of watching or listening to other people."

"No, I'm not one of them."

"I didn't really think so." Sharlene went quiet again.

"Besides Lyndsay, you're the only one that's ever been under here with me."

"I came here to tell you something, Harris."

"What?"

"I've got a job in Sydney, and I'm going to move there."

"When?"

"Tomorrow. My friend is coming over with her car to help me pack everything up."

"Do you want to go?"

"I don't know. I guess so."

"Is it a good job?"

"It's okay. I don't need much, I'm going to be staying with my friend. Her name is Kaylene."

"Is that the one who lives in the squat at Darlinghurst?"

"I forgot you read my mail. Yes, that's the one."

"I suppose you have to go."

"Will you miss me, Harris?"

"Yes."

"You could be the first one, Harris."

"I could visit you?"

"Yes, but don't tell your mum and dad it's a squat."

"Will you be all right there?"

"I'll be as okay there as I am here."

"Maybe we can write."

"And I will miss you, Harris." Sharlene leaned across the sugar and kissed me just in front of my ear, and crawled out from under the house.

Sometimes when you sit real still for a long time you can hear your heart beat, or feel it, like it's inside a drum skin. You start thinking about it and you wonder what keeps it going so steady all the time. And then you notice your breathing and it seems like it belongs to someone else, and where you never thought about it, the breathing, that is, as soon as you do, you have to take over doing it. You can't leave it on automatic any longer. I don't think we should ever think about breathing.

9

There are lots of different ways to divide people; I do it all the time. For instance there are people who, if they are walking down the street and they see a sheet of paper face down on the path, that might have something interesting on the down side, just walk past it. And then there are other people who will bend down and turn it over. Mind you once I turned over a sheet that had been used to squash a cockroach. Not all interesting things are pleasant. In my case I never did expect dead cockroaches. I expected a treasure map or a twenty-dollar note, or the key to the meaning of life or some such thing. To find out about Clementine was one of the first times I didn't want to turn the sheet over.

I rang the hospital at 6.45 a.m. the next morning. Everyone in the house was still asleep. A nurse answered and asked me to hold on. I held on for fifteen minutes and then decided she had forgotten me. I hung up and dialled again. The ward sister answered this time. She wanted to know my relationship to Clementine. I told her I was her uncle. She didn't believe me. She told me that information about patients could not be given out on the telephone. I asked for her name. She was Sister Margaret Forsythe. I asked did she have any nieces. She hung up on me.

At 7.15 a.m. I was dressed and on my way to Mrs Mac's. The back door was unlocked. It was always unlocked; Helen said that anyone who wanted to get in would only break something anyway. Clementine's room was empty. Julius was asleep. Helen was sitting up in bed smoking. I stood at the doorway to her bedroom. The clock radio was playing a "flashback", an old Beatles number. Clementine was dead.

I wanted to hold onto Mrs Mac, but I didn't. I just stood leaning against the doorway like I was waiting in a queue or something.

The Beatles song finished. I couldn't tell if Mrs Mac was looking at me or not. She was white looking, her face. And her eyes looked like a really old person's eyes that you sort of look away from. Julius pushed through the doorway past me and climbed onto his mother's bed. Mrs Mac looked at him. He was still mostly asleep. Down his legs I could see thin blue stripes of beginning bruises. Julius had been hit a lot with something thin. I thought it must have been the dowelling rod Mrs Mac used to get the pot plants down with, from the top shelf in the kitchen. He climbed into bed alongside his mother and, holding on to her, he went straight to sleep. She squashed her cigarette out.

"Did you hit Julius, for Clementine?" I asked quietly. Mrs Mac didn't answer. "It wasn't his fault," I said. "I should have been watching them properly."

The clock radio was telling us how we could win one thousand dollars by naming the last three records played, if they happened to phone us up.

"I should have done something. I should have worked it out ... " I whispered. "If I had thought about it hard enough ... "

"Go away, Harris," Mrs Mac said.

Julius sat up in bed holding onto his mother. His eyes popping too wide, he looked at me through his sleep.

10

Lyndsay's wedding service went smoothly. Jacquiline really looked very nice. Like her and her teeth had been waiting for this moment of whiteness all their lives. There were about eighty guests at the reception and they sat in two long rows at trestled tables with starched sheets for table cloths. Beer was placed on the tables in glass jugs. I think I drank about a jugful before I got my headache. I didn't usually get headaches, and I didn't usually drink jugfuls of beer. I was sitting alongside my Uncle Errol and Aunty Madeline. Uncle Errol was like a skinny combination of Bristow and Mr Magoo. I think he took out superannuation for his retirement right after he started pre-school. He is a clerk in the Department of Lands, and his job is to record where the files go. Like if a section of the department wants a file from another section then it has to go through Uncle Errol, and he marks down where it's going. You can understand why he thought about retiring all the time, when you think about it.

Aunty Madeline, my mother says, is mad. Not having children, my mother says, sends women mad. Aunty Madeline used to say "fancy" and "to think about it" and "well, what do you know", which isn't so strange, only that's just about all she ever says. She never once said anything that ever told me anything, like, "I had a game of golf today, Harris." I think Aunty Madeline is retarded. When I got my headache she said to me, "Fancy that."

"No, I don't really, Aunty Madeline," I said.

She said, "Well, what do you know."

I said, "I think I drank too much beer."

She said, "To think about it, little Harris drinking beer."

"I feel sick, Aunty," I said.

"Heavens," she said.

"We'll have our weekender paid for in three years," said Uncle Errol.

"To think about it," said Aunty Madeline.

"I think I'm going to vomit all over the table," I said.

"I could retire at sixty if I wanted to. That's next year, boy," said Uncle Errol.

"Oh, fancy that."

"I'm going to vomit all over your weekender," I said.

"Of course you can come down any time you like, after I've retired."

I said to Uncle Errol, "Your wife is an idiot."

"I can't decide to take my superannuation in a lump sum or not."

"Your husband's a moron," I said to Aunty Madeline.

"Fancy that," she said.

"Can you hear me, Uncle Errol?" I said, "You're a moron and your wife's an idiot." Something was wrong, but for a while I couldn't pick what it was. Then the silence began to seep through to me. No-one in the whole room was talking or eating or moving. Everyone was looking at me. I must have gotten very loud — even Uncle Errol looked like he could hear me. I was also standing on the table with my left foot in a salad bowl, which probably drew a bit of attention. Someone seemed to be talking to me. I held a jug of beer in my hand. It was Jacquiline, telling me something.

"Get off the table, Harris," she said.

"Get off the planet, Jacquiline," I said.

"You're being silly, Harry."

"How many teeth have you got, Jacquiline?"

"Don't be silly, Harry. Everyone is listening to you make a fool of yourself."

"I feel sick, Jacquiline."

"You've had too much to drink."

"I want to be sick on Uncle Errol and Aunty Madeline."

"Fancy that," Aunt Madeline said, and moved her chair back.

"I want to be sick on everybody," I said, an1 I must have run up the table, which is not very easy with a jug of beer in your hand, people grabbing at your ankles, and all that food. I don't think I was able to be sick on anybody, so I must have decided to tip the beer on as many people as possible. It seemed strange to me that not many people got out of the way. Some of the men were grabbing at me and others were laughing. I guess I decided I wanted to piss on everybody then, and that's when everyone stopped laughing and got out of the way very quickly. No-one was trying to grab at my ankles anymore, as I tiptoed up and down the table pissing on empty chairs and empty jugs — I had a lot of piss in me. I remember I didn't really feel drunk; more like I was angry, very angry, but all I could do was piss on things.

It was an old boyfriend of Jacquiline's, Larry Gavichon, who got me off the table. He played rugby league a lot and was called the "Angel of Death", partly because he had this tattoo on his shoulder of an angel, and partly because he used to break people's bones when he jumped on them on the football field. Larry tackled me on top of the table as I was pulling my zip back up. For a moment I knew how that cockroach felt, the one under the sheet of paper. Apparently I bit old Larry on his hairy neck (just like a vampire, they said) but it certainly got him off me real quick. Have you ever noticed how these big tough-looking guys can't take pain? The thing I know about pain is that you have to believe it's going to stop, and you keep thinking it's going to stop, not you're going to stop. In fact it's just a matter of outlasting it. I mean, I could stand this incredible pain if I knew it was only going to last one second.

With the Angel of Death, I think it would have been better to piss on him rather than chew on his neck, but I didn't have anything left. He just about ripped my head out like a paspalum weed. I had this vision of my head in Larry's hands with all my guts dangling down out of my neck, and old Larry trying to stuff them all back in again and put my head back on.

Apparently, a couple of Lyndsay's mates carried me off and locked me in a car, while all the time I kept spitting on their heads. I'm a very good spitter, as well as a pisser. I could always beat Lyndsay peeing up the wall. He used to say his was worn more than mine. We even used to have peeing fights, and I usually won, except once when Lyndsay saved his up in a tin can for a week.

The person whose car it was they locked me up in must have been pretty worried, because they said I was like a mad animal and started eating the seats. They took me out and must have decided I was something more than just drunk and locked me in the toilet, while they called for a doctor. It's pretty hard to do much to a public toilet, but apparently I did it. They told me the noise was very scary, and my father had to pay $286 damages.

11

The doctor gave me an injection which allowed them to get me home without being spat at, pissed on, or eaten. I think I slept for about two days. When I finally woke up I must have decided to go straight under the house. It was cool and dark as always. I could feel the sandstone grains jam up under my fingernails when I scraped the pounding stone clean. I always liked to start with clean sugar. Eventually I knew I would have to go and collect some more stone to crush. I hoped I could find pure white without the streaks of yellow and brown in them. But you couldn't see the colours most times, until you got inside the stone, and even then you had to take it out of the dark and look at it in the daylight. Sometimes when I couldn't be sure whether the grains were pure white or not, I wouldn't take them out in the light to find out, I would wrap them up in the dark and put them with all the rest.

Above my head, my mother was talking on the telephone. If I could have seen through the floorboards, I would have been looking up her dress. I put the thread-and-nut end of the galvanised bolt into my ear, and the rounded end onto the floorboards. She was telling someone on the phone about me. About some of the things I had been doing since the wedding; like burying the lawn mower in the garden and unscrewing the doors on my wardrobes.

"He was sitting in the garden, yesterday," she said, "and he was stirring something in our metal garbage can. It was over a little fire he had made, and I asked him what he was doing, and he said, 'I'm making paint'. I was very patient, really, I said, 'What for dear?' and he said, 'It's blackboard paint'. I said, 'What is it you're cooking, darling?' and he said, 'It's my records.' And it was. It was all his records he had been collecting since he was twelve years old." My mother sounded like she was crying at this point; there was a large pause. "And he keeps hold of this big bolt thing all the time. Yes, a bolt, that's right; a metal bolt with a nut on it. And if he doesn't want to answer you, he puts it into his ear, as if he's deaf." She sounded a bit angry now. "I try to talk to him and so does his father, but he just won't listen. We don't know what to do with him. He can't go to school like this. He's under the house right now." There was a big pause, like my mother was listening, then she said, "Yes, yes, please, oh yes, we would be very grateful if you would. Yes, tomorrow, yes, ten o'clock, yes. Thank you Mr Lehare, yes, thank you. Yes he'll be here, yes, thank you, yes, ten o'clock, yes, thank you." My mother liked to say "yes" a lot to other people.

I had quite a lot of sugar to wrap.

Sam Lehare arrived at exactly 10.00 a.m. He wore expensive clothes and told me he was a psychologist with the Health Department. We talked for a while about nothing I can remember, then he told me he had this new sort of program going for some special kids (I thought the "special" meant nuts). What he had was this cottage where these four special kids who were "emotionally disturbed" lived with him while they sorted out their problems and stuff. The cottage was actually a two-storey terrace and everyone was mostly free to do school work or go out to work. They had to meet as a group, once a week, and they had to see Sam on their own, for therapy, a couple of times a week. Everyone had to share the cleaning and other stuff, too. He didn't mention anything about the bolt I was carrying or the lawn mower, or anything.

My mother was crying when I left with Sam. I don't know what day it was, but it wasn't long after his visit. My father had his hands in his pockets. He looked a bit embarrassed. I could feel the galvanised bolt in mine. The sky was changing from sun to cloud to sun all the time. I got my old tired feeling again. My mum and dad seemed to look smaller, as if they were standing away on a distant hill or something. I think I went to sleep in the car.

*Inside my head the blue and green checked
girl threw down her school bag, and
wrenched her hand from the lady holding
it. My fingers hurt from climbing at
the chain wire. She ran back towards
me. The lady quickly followed and
caught her at the gate. Her fingers
twisted around mine in the chain wire.
There were tears running down her face,
but no sounds. Someone was pulling me
off the gate. It felt like my mother.
Someone was screaming. It was me.*

12

Sam was sitting straight in front of me in one of those old-fashioned lounge chairs with arms a mile wide. I was in one too. They make you spread your arms out as if you had no need to protect yourself from anything — like a king or prince or something.

"Tell me about yourself," Sam said.

"Why?"

"Because that's what I ask people to do when I don't know how else to start talking to them. I could say, why are you acting weird?"

"I don't know."

"Don't know what?"

"Why I'm acting weird."

"I didn't ask you that, I asked you to tell me about yourself."

"I act weird and I don't know why." He laughed a good laugh at that; one of those "not held back" ones. "You have a good laugh," I said.

"I know, I use it a lot. My wife says it's because I think that everyone believes it to be charming. She's probably right."

"It's a good laugh."

"Thank you. What is the bolt for?"

"I don't know."

"Can you let me have it for a moment?"

"No."

"Okay, tell me about the bolt, then."

"It's galvanised."

"Yes, I can see it is. Is it special for you, in any way?"

"I don't know."

"Would you like some coffee?"

"Do you have tea?"

"Sure. Your mother was telling me you got very upset at your brother's wedding."

"How come you live here and not with your wife?"

"We're separated."

"You have any children?"

"No."

Sipping tea with Sam was very pleasant. I put the bolt in my pocket. It was there if I needed it. I liked how Sam concentrated on you when he talked. No-one I ever talked to concentrated on you like Sam did. His eyes always looked at one of your eyes, not backwards and forwards from one to the other, and he never interrupted you. Sometimes he wouldn't say anything. He was the only person I ever found who knew how to be silent with somebody.

"Harris, later on I'm going to get you to do some tests, and drawings, and we'll do something called 'role-playing', where you and I might take different parts. I will explain about it at each session, and I will tell you why I am doing it, at the time. But not today. I want you to meet the other residents."

They were sitting at a long table full of food. Two boys and two girls. One of the girls was small and pretty; her name was Angela. The boys were called Marlo and Joseph. Joseph almost raped somebody once, and Marlo had these empty eyes. The other one, Stephanie, looked like a skeleton with brown canvas stretched over it. They didn't stop eating much when I was introduced, and I imagined myself away. Sam must have explained about me and my bolt because none of them commented. I sat at the end of the table alongside Angela. Sam sat opposite me. I asked Angela how old she was, but she didn't answer. Stephanie had butter stuck on the side of her mouth. She didn't seem to chew her food, she sort of pushed it down with her fingers like I used to tamp dirt down holes when I planted a tree. I felt very tired and went to my room. It was on the top floor and had a window shaped like a church's, with a shelf you could sit on if you scrunched your legs up and pressed your face against the glass. Outside were rows of similar terrace houses and backyards, and in the distance the Harbour Bridge and Centrepoint Tower lights. In one of the backyards, someone was having a barbecue; two couples. They kept laughing and talking and holding onto each other. They looked very comfortable together, like families on television, with shiny hair. I wanted to write to Mary Tyler Moore and ask her if she ever got dandruff. I wondered if this kind of thinking was what made you mad or whether you thought like this because you *were* mad. I slept for a long time.

I found out the next morning why Angela didn't answer me at the table. She doesn't answer anyone. Joseph told me that was why she was here at the cottage; because she stopped talking. Joseph told me he was here because he was over-sexed. He said it was something to do with his glands but that no-one would believe him, except maybe Sam, who never said he didn't believe him. Joseph was a very big person with oily skin and long black hair. He ate breakfast bent over his rice bubbles and the milk would dribble off the spoon every time he hauled it to his mouth.

"I'd love to screw Angela," he said.

I reached for my bolt.

"She wouldn't even yell out or anything," he dribbled.

"She is very nice," I mumbled.

"Why have you got that bolt in your ear?"

"I don't know."

"I couldn't screw Stephanie, though," he said, spitting milk onto the backs of my hands.

"She's very thin," I said.

"It'd go right through her," he said. "Do you know she vomits up after every meal? She's nuts."

"She's very thin."

"I saw her tits, once," Joseph said. "They were like ... like ... two little thumb tacks. She's all bones. Not like our Angela, I wouldn't mind getting a look at hers. What are you doing here?"

"I don't know."

"Hey, maybe you're the nut with the bolt, ha ha ha ha ha

56

ha. The nut with the bolt, get it? Ha ha ha ha.''

There is a lot of milk and rice bubbles sprayed around when Joseph laughs. Sam came in and sat down.

"What are you laughing about, Joseph?"

"I just made this little joke with Harris, Sam. I said he might be the nut with the bolt, ha ha ha, get it?"

Sam smiles and looks at me. I put the bolt in my pocket and eat my toast.

"Did you sleep okay?" Sam asks me.

"Yes, thank you," I reply. I did sleep okay, even though the traffic noise was much louder than I was used to.

"Marlo has a job at Woolworths, and Joseph goes to technical college down the road. Angela and Stephanie are still at school. They stay here the same as you do. There is a teacher who comes in Monday to Friday. You'll like her. Her name is Mrs Freeman.''

Joseph tipped the bowl up into his face to get the last bit of sugary milk. He began to wipe his face with the table cloth but looked at Sam and used a tissue instead. He said goodbye, and left.

I was left at the table with Sam.

"I would like to do some tests with you, this morning, Harris," Sam said.

The tests took all morning. I put little cards with pictures on them in a row so they told a story, and I placed blocks with triangles on them in special patterns. I drew pictures. Sam said to draw my family, but don't make them people, make them objects. I ask Sam, "Who is the nut here?" He laughs his good laugh.

We finished testing at lunchtime and we sat opposite Stephanie and Angela. Stephanie is poking a sandwich down her neck like before, and Angela doesn't look at anybody. There seemed nothing to say.

In the afternoon I met the teacher, Mrs Freeman, who wore a suit made of leather or vinyl or something. She had an accent like a Dutch kid I used to know. She got used to the bolt in my ear very quickly and stopped asking me questions. I thought to myself I should have had this bolt with me since second grade. I felt sorry for Mrs Freeman as only Stephanie would answer questions — and she mostly looked like she wanted to vomit. Stephanie kept going to the toilet a lot, which sent the lesson on a bigger nose-dive, with just me and Angela. Angela didn't mind writing though. It was just talking she didn't do. Apparently I went to sleep in the afternoon and Mrs Freeman let me.

13

Sam: Harris, what we do here is we meet once a week to talk about anything that has happened during the week that has concerned us; good, bad, or otherwise. We try to talk it over here together. The aim being to help us all cope better.
Joseph: Sam, can we get another cook?
Marlo: Yeah.
Joseph: We've had cabbage and carrots every night for a month.
Marlo: Yeah.
Sam: Maybe we could ask her to cook something different?
Marlo: Yeah, like her goose.
Joseph: Ha ha ha ha.
Sam: Why don't you ask her, Joseph?
Joseph: Not with all those meat cleavers ...
Marlo: I'll tell her, stupid bitch.
Sam: Not tell, *ask*.
Marlo: I'll ask her, then — to cook something else ... or else.
Joseph: Ha ha ha ha.
Sam: What do you think about the food, Harris?
Harris: It's okay.
Joseph: He hasn't been eating it long enough, Sam.
Marlo: Yeah, look. He's still healthy.
Joseph: Ha ha ha ha.
Stephanie: I don't like her food either.
Marlo: You don't like anyone's food.
Joseph: Ha ha ha ha.
Sam: Perhaps you could talk to her, Stephanie.
Marlo: Why don't you just get sick at the table, instead of running to the bathroom. That should get through to her.
Stephanie: It's you that makes me sick.

Marlo: You don't have to eat me ... That is, unless you want to.

Joseph: Ha ha ha ha.

Sam: How is the job going, Marlo?

Marlo: It's okay, except this little section manager, Fish-head we call him, he looks just like one, he never leaves me alone. 'Do this, Pike', 'Answer the service bell, Pike', 'Fix up the display tickets, Pike', 'Straighten your tie, Pike.'

Sam: He does this only to you?

Marlo: Yeah, the little bastard. One day I'm going to pound his fish-face in.

Joseph: You'll get sacked.

Marlo: It'll be worth it.

Sam: Have you tried talking to him?

Marlo: You can't talk to people like Fish-head. He's the kind who gets worse if you ...

Stephanie: Why don't you go to the manager?

Marlo: He wouldn't believe me. He knows where I come from.

Sam: Here, you mean?

Marlo: Yeah, they all think this is a funny farm. 'Nice coat, Pike. What do you call it, a straitjacket?'

Sam: That make you angry?

Marlo: No, of course not. I love 'em when they say 'What have you got for lunch, Pike? Fruit cake?'

Sam: What do you do when they say that?

Marlo: Nothing. I just feel nothing, and I do nothing.

Sam: You want to pay them back sometime?

Marlo: Maybe.

Sam: How are you going to do that?

Marlo: I don't know, yet.

Stephanie: Why don't you just ignore them, as if they weren't really there.

Marlo: How about you come up one day, Steph? I'll introduce you and you can throw up all over them.

Joseph: Ha ha ha ha.

Stephanie: Well you make me sick, so that part would be easy.

Sam: What do you think Marlo could do, Joe?

Joseph: Nothing, Sam. There's nothing you can do about that kind of thing.

Marlo: Maybe.

Joseph: You're best off to get used to it as soon as possible.

Sam: Accept that some people are like that?

Joseph: Yeah, they are, Sam.

Sam: All of them?

Joseph: No, there are always some of them who are okay.

Marlo: Not where I work.

Sam: Maybe you have to find them.

Marlo: I ain't found them yet.

Sam: Where do you look?

Marlo: Nowhere.

Stephanie: There aren't any there.

Marlo: Go and chunder, Stephanie.

Stephanie: Go and make everyone sick, Marlo.

Silence

Marlo: Why has he got that bolt in his ear?

Joseph: I said he must be the nut with the bolt, get it? The nut with the bolt, ha ha ha ha.

Marlo: You must be the moron with the mouth.

Joseph: Ha ha ha ha.

Stephanie: His eyes are shut.

Joseph: He's asleep.

14

Have you ever noticed how, when great things happen to you, they happen too late for you to really enjoy them? If you win some money, it never comes when you need it, but only when you've got plenty, and you say, "I could have done with this last year or whatever."

A week after Sam's testing at the cottage, he called me in to his therapy room and said, "Harris, I have some interesting news for you."

I always wish people wouldn't do that because I usually imagine something that's really a whole lot better than what they end up telling me.

"You know those tests we did? Well, it seems you have scored quite highly."

See how it happens? I was thinking of something much better than that.

"You have an above-average I.Q."

You know who I thought of just then? Miss Imperago, the old teacher that told my mother I was backward, maybe retarded. I wondered where she was. I thought I would like to send her a telegram or something.

DEAR MISS IMPERAGO,
Harris Berne former student found to have high I.Q. stop your opinion wrong stop please hand in your chalk and brief-case stop.

"Does it surprise you?" Sam asked.
"Maybe your tests are wrong."
"I don't think so. I checked them all."
"How come I'm so lousy at school?"
"I don't know, Harris. What do you think?"
"I don't know."

"Perhaps we can find out."

"Maybe."

Two nights after Sam told me I was supposed to have a high
I.Q., Marlo bundled me into his room, like one of those
resistance fighters in an old black and white war movie. Marlo
always looked like he was some kind of burglar — even in the
place he lived. I think he must have got accused a lot at some
time.

"I want to show you something," he said.

Marlo's room was really neat and tidy. He took a
wardrobe key from behind a bookshelf, opened the door and
reached into the pocket of a huge grey overcoat hanging at the
back.

"What is it?" I asked.

"Wait and I'll show you," he said.

He was very excited, and was breathing fast. I couldn't
imagine what Marlo could get excited about in the pocket of
an old coat in his wardrobe. He drew out a package wrapped
in oily cotton bandages.

"What is it?" I asked again.

"Wait on," he said. "I'll unwrap it."

He carefully unwound the bandages as if they were
covering somebody's wounds. It was dark in his room.

"Can I put the light on?" I asked.

"No," he hissed at me. "Look at this."

Marlo had uncovered a dark, shiny object that looked
like a gun.

"What is it?"

"It's a gun," he said with reverence.

"Is it a real one?"

"Of course it is."

"What's it for?"

"What do you mean?" Marlo looked at me as if I was
trying to be clever, or funny, or both.

"What have you got it for?"

"Because I might need it one day." Marlo picked it up
delicately and sighted along the barrel. "I have some bullets

too. Look." He spilled three bullets out of the gun, then slotted them back into their holes. "All you have to do is flick off the safety," he flicked off the safety catch, "and pull the trigger." He aimed the gun at my face.

"Don't do that."

"Don't worry, I'm not going to shoot you."

"Where did you get it?"

"You don't have to know that."

"I don't think you should leave it loaded."

"No-one knows it's here, except you and me."

"What did you have to show me for?"

"I'm putting it back, now."

"Put the safety catch back on."

A couple of nights later, I was talking with Angela; well, talking *to* Angela, you didn't talk *with* Angela because Angela didn't talk. She would listen, though, and she would sometimes smile and nod and move her eyebrows around so you could see what she might be thinking.

We were out in the backyard. It wasn't really a garden. It was half concreted and had a few geraniums in pots and one big gum-tree. It was after dinner, and I had sat with Angela a couple of times before. We never communicated much. Probably a lot of problems have started in the world because people have to say things to each other rather than say nothing.

In a way, Angela reminded me of Mrs Mac and Sharlene. She didn't really look like either of them but I used to sometimes call her Helen or Sharlene, and I only realised I did it if anyone else heard and they said something. I used to dream a lot, too; of this person who was all three of them mixed together, but I couldn't remember what actually happened in the dreams.

I told Angela that I wished I didn't feel so tired all the time, and she pulled her eyebrows up and her mouth across to indicate, "Well, that's not so bad", or something. Then she reached over and took the bolt from me. It was funny to see someone else holding it. She put it up to her ear and held it there for a while, as if something was going to happen. Then she turned to me and gave it back with this look on her face saying, "It probably only works for you."

Joseph came out and asked Angela if she would like to fuck. It was sort of a joke of his, to ask Angela. Angela didn't look at him.

I said, "Go fuck yourself, Joseph," and I couldn't believe I'd said it. I waited for Joseph to smash me down. Underneath, I think I might have been looking forward to it.

"I'm only joking," he said, sort of hurt-like, and he went back inside.

A week later I began to write a letter to Mrs Mac.

Dear Mrs Mac,

I should have written this to you sooner, only I don't feel so good these days. I get tired a lot.

I couldn't get past this, and I screwed it up and threw it away.

One of my regular dreams was that Helen and Julius were visiting my parents at home and Lyndsay and Jacquiline were there. I would come in and the conversation would stop and everyone would sort of ignore me, but like as if they were really conscious of me, like as if I had something all over me, or no pants on, or something, and they couldn't tell me. They would all sort of be together and start talking again and I would think that they all knew something I didn't know; something I would never know. And then I would go under the house and make sugar while the floorboards creaked and the bolt wasn't able to pick up their whispering.

Three months after coming to the cottage, I could have a first visit from my parents. One of Sam's rules was no visits from anyone for a while after coming. He explained why to me once, but I must have been listening to something else.

My mother was dressed up as if she was going to a ladies' luncheon or something. My father looked uncomfortable as usual. He had one hand in his pocket and kept looking at the door all the time.

"Your father bought you a book," my mother said. "It's about famous gardens." She rummaged in her bag. "And I brought you some fruit."

"Thanks, Mum," I said. The book must have been bought by Lyndsay or Sharlene — my father wasn't sure I could read. He shifted his weight from one leg to the other. This was an embarrassment to him, a weird son in a nuthouse. My father could always talk to Lyndsay. They used to talk about cars and engines and building things. Lyndsay was always more agreeable with my father than I ever was. He laid bricks, my father. He was very good at it, and he always had plenty of jobs. Sometimes I used to go with him and Lyndsay on a job on the weekend. He used to be very patient with me, especially when he would ask me to do something or get something. Most times I got it wrong; I never knew why. Sharlene said I used to try too hard and that I probably wasn't any good at that sort of thing anyway. Sam told me I probably did it on purpose, unconsciously he said, deliberately failing so that if he was going to love me, it would have to be for me and not for pleasing him (something like that, Sam said). I did want him to think I was good at something, but I don't think I ever knew what he really thought.

My father never talked directly to me at all. He sort of spoke to me through my mother, like she was an interpreter. Sometimes I used to think that he was more frightened of me than I was of him.

Now he stood behind my mother, who was sitting in a cane chair opposite me. He had his hand on her shoulder. He always seemed to keep some kind of contact with her. He was tall and thin and dark, with green eyes like mine, and I liked it when people used to say I looked like him. My mother was pretty fat, but had nice hair. She mostly spent her time looking after my father.

"What's the food like?" my mother asked.

"It's very good," I said.

"Why is that girl so thin?"

"Stephanie? She doesn't like eating much."

"Too well fed," my father said to my mother.

"How are you feeling, Harris?" my mother asked.

"Good, Mum. I'm feeling really good."

"Your mother has been worrying herself sick," my father said, looking at my mother.

"I'm sorry, Mum."

"It's my ulcer."

"The doctor said she's not to be upset," said my father. "She's got four different medicines to take."

"Your father's not well either," said my mother.

"I'm all right."

"You're not," she said. "He had pains in the chest, and I took him to the doctor's surgery at about midnight, and woke the doctor up to have a look at him. He said it could have been a small heart attack. He works too hard. Have you taken your heart pill?"

"Yes, I took it in the car. Didn't I?"

"I should have brought my antacid."

"How's Sharlene?" I asked.

"We haven't heard from her since she left. I wrote to the address she gave us, but the letter came back," my mother said. "I don't think she wants to hear from us."

"She telephoned us up, one night," my father said, "to tell us she was all right. I had to make your mother hang up — she was only getting upset."

"I think it's bad seed. Your Aunty Kathleen was never any good, and I did try so hard with Sharlene."

"Don't go getting upset, now."

"Maybe it's my fault," said my mother.

"Don't be silly," said my father.

"What did we do wrong? Sharlene and Harris and ..."
My mother was crying.

"You didn't do anything wrong, Mum."

"Well, we tried," my father said.

"How's Lyndsay?" I asked.

My mother blew her nose and stopped crying. "Oh, their place is looking so nice. Lyndsay's worked so hard, and Jacquiline, too. They haven't got much furniture yet, but

Lyndsay's got a second job selling spare parts on the weekend. Jacquiline wants to have a baby very soon, as soon as they get the carpet paid for."

At that moment, I looked at my father and for once our eyes met. For the first time in my life, I felt sorry for him. He looked like a kid, and for some reason I felt older and wiser than him. He looked trapped and bewildered.

"Lyndsay's doing very well," he said without much conviction.

"Jacquiline's like a daughter to me," my mother said. "She comes down twice a week and helps me do the ironing and cooking."

"She's a real help to your mother," my father said absently.

"Lyndsay's so lucky to have got her."

"What happened about that Forest Ranger thing?" my father asked.

"I don't know. I suppose when I didn't show up they got someone else."

"Maybe you can still get into it?" he said.

"You know Mrs Beckhouse's dog?" my mother said. "It got run over the other night."

"Well, at least it won't be tied up and barking every day," said my father.

I could feel my tiredness coming on. Then my father surprised me. He said, "I hope you get to be a Forest Ranger."

"I suppose we will have to go," my mother said.

"You can stay longer, if you want."

"Better to go ahead of the peak-hour traffic."

"Your mother gets nervous in the traffic."

"I don't think it's good for your father to have all that tension — everyone changing lanes all the time."

"Some idiot passed us at a hundred miles an hour on the wrong side of the double lines ..."

"Are you sure you get enough to eat?"

"Yes, Mum."

"I'll ring up next week."

"Okay."

My father didn't know whether to shake my hand or not. He looked at me and then decided not to. My mother was looking teary-eyed.

"Don't go getting upset," he said.

"You tell them if you get hungry."

"Yes, Mum. Goodbye."

"Goodbye, Harris."

15

On Saturday night, Sam had gone away for the weekend and left a husband and wife team, Shirley and Franklyn, in charge. Shirley and Frank liked to drink and watch T.V. a lot in their room. I don't think Sam knew what lousy minders Shirley and Frank were. Joseph and Marlo decided to have an illegal night out, and to take me. Joseph sat on the end of my bed and tried to whisper, but like everything else with Joseph, he couldn't control it. Marlo told him to shut up, twenty times, but after a while we realised that Frank and Shirley must be too drunk to hear. Joseph took the bolt from me and put it under my bed.

Marlo climbed out my window and clung to the plastic sewer pipe as he dangled his way down to the ground. I went after Joseph, thinking that if it holds him it will certainly hold me. I waited for his oily face to hit the concrete with plastic sewer pipe and shit falling all around him, but all I heard was the squeaky sound of flesh sliding over plastic. I followed him down, wanting to go to the toilet and cutting my hand on a bracket screw.

I had not been away from the cottage since I'd come here, except once to go shopping with Sam. The city lights looked good in the air.

Marlo took charge. He had most of the money, and he always seemed to know what he didn't want to do. Marlo didn't want to catch a bus, so we travelled by taxi to Kings Cross. It was ten o'clock and the streets were packed. Marlo took us into a corner hotel, where the barmaids wore plastic see-through blouses and the smoke wouldn't sink in the air. He ordered three Bacardi and Cokes and got very embarrassed when he had to reach for more money than he first gave the waitress. She smiled at him though, and he gave her a big tip.

Joseph swallowed his drink immediately and kept pointing at plastic blouses that held bigger and bigger tits.

In a corner of the lounge, a band was playing something that almost sounded like music. A blonde singer was chewing into a microphone that "Love was a gift from heaven" — you couldn't help thinking that talent was too. Marlo bought three beers from the same waitress, who leaned so far over the table that Joseph almost fogged up her blouse.

A couple of tables over, there were three girls sitting by themselves. They looked bored and not much older than us.

"I'm having the middle one," Joseph said.

"You can ask them, then," Marlo said.

"You go ask them, Harris," Joseph finished his beer. "Ask them whether they would like to join us, or we could join them."

"I'll ask them," Marlo crinkled his empty eyes, but you could see fear in them. Marlo was the kind of person that made himself do things, especially if he was afraid. Like he needed everyone to believe that what he did was what he was, and you knew that he wanted to believe it more than anyone. As he walked over to their table, I could feel a sort of admiration. I couldn't have done it myself. Marlo was crouched down at their table, and the three of them looked over at Joseph and me. Joseph smiled and my stomach dropped. I was waiting for my tired feeling, but it didn't come. Marlo came back to our table.

"Come on, bring your drinks; the one on the left side is mine."

The one on the left side was Marjorie, the one in the middle was Sondra, and the other was Rosalie. Rosalie looked like she had had some childhood disease that's supposed to kill you. She definitely looked more dead than alive. Sondra kept farting all the time. At least I think it was Sondra; she kept making lots of noise with her straw. Marjorie was blinking all the time. I think she had her mother's eyelashes on and the weight was a bit much. Marlo bought three more beers and three long coloured drinks you see on travel posters for Fiji or Bali.

The blonde singer was telling us that "Her man left her in Dallas". I figured no-one here would be too surprised. Marjorie was telling us that they came here all the time. Joseph was trying to look down Sondra's front and Rosalie looked more like those patients on television when the little green radar bleep runs straight across the screen. Everyone was having a good time.

Marlo was telling them how his car was in the garage after an accident with a police car, and that his flat was being treated by pest exterminators (so we couldn't go there). Marlo is a really great liar. I was beginning to believe him myself. I asked Rosalie did she feel all right. Apparently she did, although Sondra had to answer for her.

"What's that smell?" Joseph wrinkled his face. Sondra slurped harder on her straw. Joseph was his usual subtle self. "Smell's like something just died." Sondra swallowed her straw and half the fruit salad floating on top of her drink.

Marlo said to forgive Joseph as he's only let out once a week. The girls giggled at this, except Rosalie, who gave more of a rattle.

Marlo asked Marjorie to dance, and she followed him on to the floor in front of the band. Joseph grabbed Sondra's arm and followed Marlo, as he panicked at the thought of being left with Rosalie. Rosalie and I were left staring at each other.

"You come here a lot?" she asked.

"Never been here before," I said. "You come here a lot?"

"Yes. I'm not supposed to, it's bad for my asthma."

"You get asthma?"

"Yes, I have to use this spray if I get an attack." She pulled a spray tube thing out of her purse. "It's the smoke that gets me." I think to myself that the smoke has already got her.

"You want to dance?" I asked.

"No, I can't dance here, I'd get an attack."

"How often do you get an attack?"

"Oh it depends if I get excited or upset or something,

and if there's lots of smoke in the air."

"Jesus, that's tough."

"I'm used to it really. My sister died of an asthma attack."

"Shit."

"She was only a baby, though."

"Do you want another drink?"

"No, I get dizzy if I drink too much."

I thought I could feel my tired feeling coming. I watched Marlo and Marjorie dancing. They didn't seem to move much, and Marlo had his eyes shut. Joseph must have had an iron grip on Sondra, as her dress was bunched up at the back. I wondered if she would clear the floor with her farting problem.

The music stopped and everyone sat down again.

Marjorie was flapping her mother's eyelashes at Marlo and telling him about her job at the Lebanese take-away, and how she had to stop the boss doing things to her when she bent over the tubs making tabouli.

Three dances later, which covered the history of asthma, the right and wrong way to make homus, and how drinking makes you sick, Marjorie said, why didn't we all go to Rosalie's place, because her parents weren't home. Joseph showed his approval by stopping his plastic-blouse staring and Sondra by stopping farting. Rosalie wasn't too keen.

"What if they come home early?" she said.

"They won't come home early," said Marjorie.

"You know what my dad's like," said Rosalie.

"What is your dad like?" I asked.

"He's very big," said Sondra, who held her hand up way over her head, and farted.

"He doesn't like boys," said Rosalie.

I could feel my tired feeling waiting in the wings.

Rosalie's house was better than I expected. It was small, white, neat, and smelled of carpet freshener and Pine-O-Clean. She was supposed to be at home in bed looking after her asthma. Marjorie found some records and put them on the stereo. Sondra and Joseph got on the lounge and started kissing. Marlo began dancing very close to Marjorie, while Rosalie did something with her nose and her asthma spray. The music had no words, but was okay to listen to. The room was warm and I could feel the comfortable effect of the drinks. I asked Rosalie if she wanted to dance when she finished with her nose. She was very stiff to dance with and obviously didn't like to touch bodies. There was nothing I could do to stop the feeling that I was floating somewhere up around the ceiling, looking down at everyone in the room. I felt sorry for Rosalie. My tired feeling was coming.

The person I wanted to see was Helen — Mrs Mac. I didn't actually want to say anything special to her, I just wanted to be with her. I wondered what she would be doing now; probably reading. She used to read till very late at night. Occasionally she would give me one of her books to read. My favourite one was called *The Committee*. It was about this committee of five that made all these decisions, and they were really inside the head of the president of America. Like they were all different types of people within the one person, and they were always trying to get their way. I had to read it twice to really understand it properly. Mrs Mac always made me feel good no matter what we were doing. I would really have liked even one minute with her, then.

Rosalie asked me if I would like some coffee and we went into the kitchen. When we came out of the kitchen, Joseph had his hand up Sondra's dress, Marlo and Marjorie were lying on the floor behind the lounge, and Rosalie's parents walked in.

He was one of the biggest men I have ever seen. Rosalie's father, that is. He sort of blinked a few times, strode over to Joseph, grabbed his throat and his active hand, and virtually threw him through the doorway with this roaring noise. I went through the kitchen and out the back door, while Rosalie's mother screamed about bitches and dogs in heat and something about the neighbours. I ran around to the front of the house and saw Marlo climb out of a window. Rosalie's father looked like he could crush things, but didn't look like he could run too fast, so Marlo stuck his fingers up at him. That was when he reappeared in the doorway holding a huge shotgun.

The three of us ran so fast we must have looked like those cartoon dogs whose feet spin on the spot before they take off. I kept listening for a gunshot and preparing my body for pain, but no shot came. We ran for ten minutes in darkness, and finally stopped under a light pole.

"Christ, is he coming?" Joseph looked back into the dark.

"I can't run anymore," Marlo said.

"They were right," Joseph shook his head.

"About what?" asked Marlo.

"He is very big."

"And he doesn't like boys," I said.

Joseph and Marlo and I started laughing. Marlo pretended to be Rosalie's father by grabbing Joseph by the neck and giving an imitation roar. Joseph almost pissed himself, and we laughed for five solid minutes, standing under the light pole, until a lady came out and told us she had just rung the police.

16

Sam: It seems the three of you broke the rules last night.
Marlo: How did you know that?
Sam: It's not important how I know.
Joseph: Couldn't have been Frank and Shirley, they were ...
Sam: It wasn't Frank and Shirley.
Marlo: It was all right, Sam, we only had two drinks each and then we came home.
Joseph: Yeah, that's right, Sam.
Sam: That's bullshit.
Marlo: What?
Sam: You did more than that.
Joseph: We did meet some nice girls.
Marlo: But we ...
Sam: What happened, Harris?
Harris: We had some drinks at the hotel and then we met these three girls who invited us ...
Marlo: Yeah, and we went to one of the girls' places, and danced for a while and then came home.
Sam: Were they alone?
Marlo: No, the parents were there.
Stephanie: You wouldn't have been there if they were.
Marlo: Shut up, Stephanie.
Sam: What else happened?
Joseph: Nothing, Sam.
Marlo: That's right, Sam, we just came home.
Sam: I was watching.
Marlo: What?
Sam: I was watching you. I followed you. I came back for my chequebook and saw you climbing out the window.
Joseph: Holy shit.

Marlo: You followed us?
Sam: Yes.
Marlo: All night?
Sam: Yes.
Joseph: You saw everything?
Sam: Probably not.
Marlo: You saw Rosalie's father?
Sam: Yes.
Joseph: He's very big, isn't he, Sam?
Marlo: We didn't think that was going to happen.
Sam: You could have been shot.
Joseph: I'm sorry, Sam.
Marlo: Me too.
Stephanie: Pity you weren't shot.
Marlo: Is that the 'fat lady' talking?
Joseph: Ha ha ha ha.
Stephanie: Is that the 'fat head' talking?
Joseph: Ha ha ha ha.
Silence
Sam: Stephanie, you've lost weight this week. In fact you've lost the last three weeks' gain.
Marlo: She's gonna be invisible.
Stephanie: I'm sorry, Sam.
Sam: Has anything happened this week?
Stephanie: Not really.
Sam: Are you missing home?
Stephanie: I don't think so.
Silence
Sam: How are you getting along with your section manager?
Marlo: Fish-head?
Sam: Yes.
Marlo: The other day he deliberately changed all the price tickets on my section when the store manager was on his rounds.
Sam: Sounds like he has something against you.
Marlo: I don't know what, Sam, I really don't know. Right from the start he's been like that. I never did one thing to him.
Sam: Maybe you haven't been respectful or polite enough?

Marlo: Jesus, Sam, I'm not going to lick his boots or kiss his bum.

Silence

Joseph: Hey, Harris has gone to sleep again.

Silence

Marlo: He's all right, you know, Sam.

Sam: Who?

Marlo: Harris.

17

I was sitting on the floor of my room playing chess with myself, which can be very confusing. What I used to do was — I'd be white until I started to lose, then I'd be black. I used to wonder whether I'd ever be any good in a war or something — I figured I'd have to have the other side's uniform underneath my clothes in case my side started going downhill. Imagine every soldier doing that, no-one would ever lose a battle. I got a picture of all these soldiers dressing and undressing on this battlefield, when Mrs Mac knocked on my door. I have often been very glad that other people can't see what goes on in my head.

I just looked at her for a while. Her eyes weren't old any-more; they were more like they used to be — deep dark brown, with the white parts very white. There was something different about her, though. She seemed smaller.

"Hullo, Harris," she said. "Are you winning?"

For a second I forgot about the chess and I thought she meant in life — the winning, that is. "I don't know," I said.

"I meant the chess game."

"Oh that," I said, "I'm just about to be black."

She laughed and sat on the floor opposite me, shaking her head at the chessboard. My bolt is on the floor near the chessboard, but I don't pick it up. "You look smaller," I said.

"I've lost some weight."

"How is Julius?"

"He's fine."

"Where is he?"

"He's staying the weekend at his grandmother's."

"Would you like a game?"

"No, I thought we might have a picnic-lunch together. I

asked Mr Lehare. He said it would be okay. I told him I was your aunt. We could go to the Botanic Gardens."

The Botanic Gardens has this giant glass pyramid full of tropical plants that have to be kept at the same temperature all year. You can climb up these iron stairs right through the greenery. The smell there is the plant equivalent of body sweat, a sort of ancient ground smell. I had been there once before on a school excursion but it wasn't any fun because you had to fill out the names of the plants on a stencilled sheet to prove you weren't having a good time.

We climbed around the pyramid for a while and then we sat on the grass near the pond. Helen is this really thoughtful kind of person with food. She taught me how to mix tastes. She once made me this sandwich; rye bread with cream cheese, smoked salmon, avocado and black caviar. It was my favourite, and you had to wash it down with icy bitter lemon.

Helen spread a ton of this stuff out on little plates on the rug and said, "Let's get fat." The sun was shining and there was just enough breeze for the seagulls to glide against. Helen's black fly-away hair was fluttering. I could taste the salmon with my tongue and feel the bite of the bitter lemon. A little way from us there was a couple who must have been in love — they kept touching each other and kissing and smiling as if no-one else was around. I think a garden is also a good place to be in love in. I thought of Mrs Mac's garden.

"How's the garden?" I said.

"I don't know, Harris. I left the house about three weeks ago."

"Where do you live now?"

"Would you believe at the back of a bookshop. I own a little bookshop in Chippendale." She clapped her hands together with enthusiasm. "Would you like to see it?"

"Yes," I said, "I really would."

"I want to go for a long walk first, and then we are going to buy something for your very drab room. A picture or something. Okay?"

"Okay."

"Something cheap. Okay?"

"Okay."

We put the picnic things in Mrs Mac's car and walked beside the sea wall that traces around Farm Cove to Mrs Macquarie's Chair. For a while our arms were sort of bumping as we walked and then somehow we were holding hands. It felt very comfortable.

"How is Frank?" I asked.

"Frank is dead."

"Oh shit," was all I could manage.

"He was in hospital with alcoholic liver disease. Frank died of an accumulation of liver collapse, pneumonia, and not wanting to live any longer."

"I'm sorry."

"Look at those sailing boats out there. We could go sailing one day."

"I don't know how to sail."

"Neither do I, but it can't be too difficult or they'd be having more accidents out there. Look at that beautiful big one there."

"Do you miss him?"

"No."

"You feel bad?"

"At first I did. I felt really sick. I felt I shouldn't have left him, that I should have tried harder to get him to stop drinking; perhaps if I'd stayed with him. After a while that didn't seem to be true. I think Frank was on a self-destruct spiral long before I ever knew him."

"Let's have a ferry ride," I said.

"Okay," she smiled.

I knew you were supposed to feel love in your heart, but when Helen smiled at me I felt this sort of wobble more in my stomach. I read this article once that described love as a collection of emotional attachments — like invisible umbilical cords between people. I often thought about that article; people sort of shooting out these quivering attempts at attaching to each other, like snails' antennae. I think I got it in the stomach; the emotional attachments, I mean.

The ferry took us to Manly. It was fairly smooth, so we sat outside and pointed at boats and little bays and harbour mansions. On the way back this really sun-tanned, muscly guy sat down alongside Helen. He was wearing shorts like P.E. teachers wear, about two sizes too small, and he looked like he carried his tennis balls around in there (maybe his racquet too). He kept moving his great hairy, brown leg up against Helen's. Even I could see this, and she quietly moved away. At first I got real angry to myself about this, but I don't swim all that great, so I didn't say anything. Then I realised that Helen was practically getting into my lap to avoid this creep, so I figured he's not all bad. I gave him this huge, big wink, like he'd just done me a fantastic favour. His face got a real shock out of this and I could see a few people around us had caught on. He stared at Helen and me with this look that said "How can she prefer that wimp to me?". He got up real embarrassed, like he just remembered something, and as soon as he'd gone, Helen and I laughed out loud together, and I could see everyone around us smiling approval. I think most people liked watching us together.

Down George Street we went into a gallery and some print shops, looking for my room brightener. We finally settled on this painting that had dozens of little people in it, that looked like they'd been painted by a kid. I knew that it was done by a "naïf" painter because I got very interested in them in art classes. I think because I felt they weren't trying to *be* anything, the naïf painters, that is, and that maybe even I could paint like that. It always looked easy to do. In this picture, the perspective was really off, and there were all these flat little people in a city street leaning on fences, talking or delivering milk or building something, and the kids in it were skipping or tossing a ball around. Everyone was doing something with someone else. No-one was doing anything by themselves. I always think I'd like to know the person who painted pictures like that.

"You carry it," Helen said to me. "Let's go see my bookshop."

The front window of the bookshop was tiny and full of paperbacks. Inside it seemed even smaller because it was jam-packed full of books. You almost had to keep your arms up in the air to sidle down the aisle. Helen's face was glowing as soon as we entered.

"What do you think?" she asked.

"It's great."

"It's terrific, isn't it?" She looked around.

"Pity no-one can get in to buy anything." Helen pretended to throw a book at me.

"Can you smell that smell?" she asked with her eyes shut. There was a Lebanese take-away next door, but I didn't think that was the smell she meant. "That's book smells," she said. I held my nose, and she laughed. "Come on out the back and see where we live."

Out the back was a big kitchen and upstairs there was a dining-room and two bedrooms. It looked pretty dark, with that Italian kind of wallpaper of gold and brown and green.

"I'll get it fixed up eventually," she said with her face screwed up as if she was spitting something sour off her tongue. "Would you like a cup of tea?"

"You sound like my mother," I said.

We sat at the kitchen table. I told her she could do with a few room brighteners herself. She told me her plans for the shop. About how she was going to start a book club and a newsletter and have reading nights. She got all excited telling me this, and talked very fast. I love to watch people get excited about things. I sort of catch some of the energy or something and I get excited right along with them. With Helen I just wanted to hold onto her very quietly so I could hear her heartbeat and feel her breathing, and maybe catch some of whatever it was she was bubbling around with. I told her about everyone at the cottage and she listened carefully. She said they all sounded a bit sad. I hadn't thought of them as sad until Helen said it. I wondered if I sounded sad too. I think most people wouldn't think of themselves as sad but a lot of them probably are.

Helen rang the cottage and okayed it with Sam for me to come back later, after dinner.

Late in the afternoon we took it in turns to read to each other from a book of short stories about these people in a village in northern Greece. I didn't read as good as she did, but it didn't matter. I never loved anything more than the two of us doing that.

Back at the cottage, lying on my back in bed, I ran the day through my head like a video. I didn't feel one bit tired.

18

I was hanging my naïf painting the next morning when Marlo slid into my room. I couldn't help feeling that Marlo would get called up a lot for police questioning before he was through. He definitely had a suspect's look. He shut the door silently and dismissed my picture with a glance.

"I got sacked yesterday," he whispered. I looked at him for a few seconds while the meaning was coming through to me. "I had a disagreement with Fish-head."

"The section manager?" I said.

"Yeah."

"They sacked you for disagreeing with him?"

"Yeah. I disagreed with him a lot."

"What did they say to you?"

"They said I shouldn't have disagreed with him by twisting a coathanger around his neck until his face went blue."

"Did you do that?"

"No, I'm only kidding. I wanted to though. I wanted to twist it around his neck till it cut into his throat and his eyes popped out. He's too big, the mongrel. No, they sacked me because they said I wasn't cut out for this kind of work. It really shits me off that they were trying to be kind. If they had said I was sacked because I was rude to customers, or I wouldn't follow orders, I wouldn't have minded. But Jesus, when they're kind to you, you know you're bloody hopeless at a job you don't even want."

"Aren't you any good?" I asked.

"I don't think so. I did try hard, you know. I'm going to tell the others they sacked me because I got in a fight with Fish-head."

"What are you going to do now?"

"I know it was Fish-head who really got me the sack. He was grinning like a hyena after I came down on the floor. He knew, the mongrel. I hate that bastard. Jesus, Harris, sometimes I think about killing him. I think about it at night, watching him beg me not to kill him. I don't dream it, I lie there and I kill him over and over." Marlo was staring through my picture with his eyes squeezed and his mouth curled up. "I could kill him so easily. I could shoot him in the face, and smash his head in. I can see him begging me, but I hold the gun up to his forehead." Marlo pulled his secret gun from out of his pocket.

"Shit, Marlo, put it away. What are you doing with it?" He turned around to face me with the gun still pointed in front of him. "Don't point it at me, Marlo." Marlo is looking at me but he isn't focused on me, he's sort of focused on something a long way off behind me. I get this picture of myself with a hole in my forehead, and the bullet has gone through my painting and even in this flash I am very angry with Marlo for putting a hole in my painting. I think I am easily as mad as Marlo.

"Don't point the gun at me, Marlo. I'm Harris, you'll ruin my painting."

"What?"

"For shit's sake, don't shoot me and my painting." Marlo begins to look like he can see me again.

"What painting?"

I point to my picture. "This one. You looked like you were going to shoot it."

"I wasn't going to shoot your painting."

"Put the gun away then."

"I brought it with me to give it to you."

"I don't want it."

"Please, Harris, you take it."

"I don't want it."

"You take it and hide it in your room so I can't find it. I can't use it if I can't find it, can I?"

"Jesus, Marlo, you're weird."

"So are you."

"But you're bloody weirder."

"What about your bolt?"

"It doesn't fire bullets."

"Well that just makes you weirder. I'll bet there are more people with guns to their heads than bloody galvanised bolts."

Now this seemed pretty funny at the time and we both fell on the bed laughing. Marlo snatched my bolt and pretended to shoot me with it and then my picture. Sometimes stupid things are really hilarious.

When we stopped laughing, I took Marlo's gun and told him I'd hide it in my room. Actually I was a fair bit scared when he pointed the gun at me. My father taught me that you should never point a gun at anyone, anytime. I don't think my father would have been a very good soldier either.

Marlo was still standing in my doorway looking at my picture. "Nice picture," he said.

"Yes."

"I'm going to go soon."

"Where?"

"Queensland; the Gold Coast."

"Does Sam know?"

"No, he'd try to stop me. I'll get a job. There's more jobs up there than down here."

"Have you got money?"

"I've got heaps. I've been saving for a year. There's nothing much to spend it on here." Marlo said all this while he was looking at my picture and drumming his fingers on the wall like horses' hooves in a cowboy movie. "Do you want to come too?" he said. I knew it cost him a lot to ask.

"No. Thanks anyway," I said.

"Yeah. Well, make sure you hide the gun properly."

"I will."

"Hey, I'll write you a letter when I get there in case you change your mind."

"Okay," I said.

"I'll see you around," he said.

"I'll see ya, Marlo," I said.

When Marlo left I took the three bullets out of the gun and sticky-taped them to the outside of it. I sat the gun in this pouch thing on the inside door of my wardrobe. I think the pouch was meant for socks and belts or something.

19

Sam told us one breakfast time that the regional director of the Health Department and a television film crew were going to visit the cottage on Saturday because it was Youth Week, and the idea of getting people out of institutions and into smaller places like our cottage was very fashionable. Mr Redman, the director, was thinking of going into politics. Sam wasn't going to be there — fortunately for him he would be away speaking at a conference on the effect of television on creativity or something. Sam asked us to make a good impression on Mr Redman.

Mr Redman introduced himself as Alec, his assistant regional director as Brendan McCarthy, and his secretary as Beverley. Alec Redman held onto your shoulder and spoke right into your face like he was going to sell you his mother's old underwear as antiques, or something. But you got the feeling that for an extra two dollars you'd get his mother in them. He smelt like a men's perfume they advertise on television where these paratroopers land and then spray themselves with this stuff, and these raving beauties leap out from behind trees and rocks and fling themselves at them. Mind you if I just jumped out of a plane, I'd definitely need some perfume before any girl would be able to come near me.

This is what happens:

Old Alec keeps asking Beverley how he looks. When he asks us a question he doesn't wait for an answer. He writes our names on pieces of paper and places them on the table in front of us. He gets the nod from the cameraman and puts on his selling face. He goes into this long speech into the camera about adolescents and the crime rate, and the great job the Government is doing getting unfortunate people out of institutions. He goes on about how he's been talking to "these kids here in the Government's cottage program". Here he makes a bit of a mistake. He grabs Angela's shoulder, looks into her face, and says, "Can you tell us something about cottage life . . . ," he looks at the paper in front of Angela with her name on it, "er, Angela?" Angela's mouth, in fact her whole face, doesn't even move for at least a minute and a half. She looks back at Mr Redman as though she doesn't approve of anyone selling anyone's underwear, let alone your mother's. Old Alec keeps his face smiling at the camera and just his eyes slide sideways to poor old Brendan to "for God's sake do something". Brendan looks as if he wants to punch Angela. He tells the cameraman to stop filming. Beverley tells Alec he still looks good, and Alec lets Angela's shoulder go and wipes the hand as if it was Angela's shoulder that was sweating.

Within minutes Mr Redman makes his second mistake. He grabs my shoulder. The cameras roll, Beverley and Brendan smile encouragement at him. He starts his speech again, then swings his face at me just as the camera closes in. The camera and the face together must have overwhelmed me because I automatically reached for my bolt. Old Alec freezes, his eyes go out to Brendan and he whispers out of the side of his mouth, "What the hell is the kid doing, Brendan?"

"He seems to be putting a bolt in his ear, Mr Redman," Brendan whispers back.

"Is he all right?"

"We could get the camera to come from the other side?"

"No the kid's a . . . not well. We'll try another one."

Mr Redman looks hard at Joseph and Stephanie and decides Joseph is his best bet. Beverley comes over and whispers something in his ear and he says, "All right just this once". Alec tells the cameraman that he, *and Beverley*, will be in the next shot with Joseph. He mutters to Beverley between his teeth as he takes Joseph's shoulder, "At last a frigging normal one". The cameras roll and we sit through old Redman's speech once more. "Well son," he says to Joseph, "how do you like it here?"

"It's very good," says Joseph. Beverley shifts up and down a bit and tries to wriggle forwards. Mr Redman glares at her when the camera moves off him.

"Would you prefer this kind of homely life to an institution?"

"Oh yes," says Joseph. Beverley squirms some more and old Alec squints angrily at her again.

I walk around behind the three of them and see Joseph's hand firmly grappling with Beverley's rear end. Joseph, then, must have grappled a little bit too hard, because Beverley drops her clipboard and reaches for her bottom. The cameraman stops without even having to be told.

Mr Redman has a glass of water with two Disprins in it and peers through the glass at Stephanie. "What's your name, dear?" he says very gently to her.

"Stephanie Anne Dawe," Stephanie says.

"How do you like it here?" he asks carefully.

"Oh I really love it here, Mr Redman. We're all like a big family here and Sam — that's Mr Lehare — he's so good with us all. I came from a big hospital to this cottage and I just love it."

"That's lovely to hear." Mr Redman turns to Beverley and Brendan, like to say he should have had this skinny one first, before those other weirdos. He asks Beverley how he looks, she straightens his tie and smooths down a couple of his eyebrow hairs that stick out. You can see he feels in charge again. He nods at the cameraman, grabs Stephanie's shoulder and swings his face into at least a kilo of Stephanie's vomit. Stephanie's thin body is very sensitive about being touched.

When Sam asked us how the filming went, we told him to wait until he sees it.

20

About two weeks after Marlo left I got a letter from him. Before I could open it Stephanie passed out in the kitchen. She sort of fell into Angela's lap at the table. For a tiny second I just sat there looking at how unusual the two of them looked — Stephanie unconscious in Angela's lap, Angela with a spoon near her mouth and her eyes really wide and frightened. I knew you were supposed to get the person's head down, to get the blood into it. I got Stephanie's head out of Angela's lap and down on the floor. I wasn't sure about mouth-to-mouth resuscitation. I kept thinking about Stephanie and her vomiting. I put my ear near her mouth until I could hear her breathing. Angela was really frightened. She held onto my arm very tight until Stephanie opened her eyes. I noticed then just how skinny Stephanie was, like her arms and legs could snap off between your fingers like stalks on a dried plant.

"I'm all right," Stephanie sighed. Angela was still clinging to my arm. "I used to faint at home all the time," she said. Angela began crying.

"Do you want to sit up?"

"In a minute," she said. Angela kept hold of my arm while she was crying. The tears seemed to be more than Stephanie's fainting deserved.

When someone cries I always get this real helpless feeling that there is something very important to be done but I can't do it; like the person needs me to do something, but I can't do it. We just sat there around Stephanie watching her breathe.

Would you believe Jacquiline and Lyndsay walked into the kitchen then. Jacquiline beamed her teeth at us on the floor. She is the only person I can imagine who could actually smile at three people on a kitchen floor, when one is half-unconscious, one is crying and the other one has a bolt in his ear. When Angela let go of my arm and Stephanie sat back in her chair, I took Lyndsay and Jacquiline to my room.

"That's a very nice painting, Harry," Jacquiline said. "Did one of your friends here do it?"

"How are you going, Hassa?" Lyndsay said.

"Good," I answered. "How's the house going?"

"Oh it's lovely," Jacquiline said. "We haven't got much furniture yet, but the carpet is paid for and I think I might be pregnant soon."

"You could help us design the garden when you get out of here, if you like," Lyndsay said.

"How are mum and dad?" I asked.

"They're fine. I see your mother twice a week. We go shopping together and I help with the ironing and cleaning," Jacquiline said.

"You ever see Mrs Soo in Greening Hills?"

"Who?"

"Mrs Wang Htsu from Vietnam. I used to mow her lawn."

"No. We're going to have kikuyu turf delivered for our lawn," Jacquiline said.

"How's your mother, Jacquiline?"

"She's fine."

"She still at the Pizza Hut?"

"Yes. Perhaps you could come and stay with us when they let you out of here."

"She still give you free Pepsis?"

"I always paid for mine," said Jacquiline.

"How's the garage?" I said to Lyndsay.

"Lyndsay doesn't work there anymore," Jacquiline answered.

"How come?"

Jacquiline lined her teeth up at me. "A friend of my uncle owns a chain of car accessory shops and Lyndsay works for him. The pay is very good and Lyndsay wears a suit ..."

"What do you do?" I asked Lyndsay.

"He's their sales manager," Jacquiline answered.

93

Lyndsay looked embarrassed.

"Sales*man*, actually. I'm the only one."

"What happened to the idea for your own garage?"

"I can always do that later on."

"What happened to the money you saved?"

"It had to go into the deposit for the house," Jacquiline said.

"Do you like being a salesman?" I asked Lyndsay.

"It's okay."

"You don't like it," I said.

"It's okay."

"You'd rather be working on cars."

"Maybe."

"Why don't you go back to the garage?"

"We can't afford to do that, Harry," Jacquiline said.

"Give up the kikuyu turf."

"Can you put that bolt down and grow up for once," Jacquiline said.

"He's going to be unhappy, Jacquiline."

"You're the one who is unhappy."

"It's going to make him unhappy."

"Look at you, you're the one who is unhappy . . . you . . . you ruiner!"

"Come on you two, calm down," Lyndsay said.

"He is, he's a ruiner. He ruined my wedding reception, he's ruining his life, and now he wants to ruin ours." Jacquiline was close to tears, her face was hot and her hands were tight little fists.

"He's not well at the moment, Jacq."

"He's never been well, he's never been normal or nice to me, not once, ever. I'm sick of him. I've tried a thousand times to be nice to him, and now he's going to turn you against me . . ."

"I think we'd better go," Lyndsay tried to smile at me. "I'll see ya, mate."

"I'll see ya, Lyndsay. See ya, Jacquiline."

At different times I've wondered whether it would be better to arrange all your bad things to happen on the one day, say every week, rather than spread them a few at a time over the whole week, if you had the choice, that is. This could have been that day for me, and it wasn't even lunchtime yet.

Actually what Jacquiline said to me sort of stung a bit and I know there has to be some truth in stuff that hurts otherwise you don't feel anything. Maybe I was a ruiner. I certainly stuffed up her wedding reception, and I wasn't doing too well anywhere in my own life. Fortunately, I remembered Marlo's letter in my pocket, and I flopped out on my bed and opened it.

11/116 BOULEVARDE AVE.,
SURFER'S PARADISE. QLD

DEAR HARRIS,

I haven't got a job yet because I am having a holiday first. This place is incredible. There are fantastic chicks everywhere, just waiting to get screwed. By the way I have included $50 in case you change your mind and want to come up. Just send me a telegram and I'll meet you. When I get a job I'm going to buy a car. You could easily stay with me. The flat I am renting is old but it has two bedrooms. I go swimming nearly every day.

The other day, on the beach, I saw an old school-teacher I used to have in primary school, Mr Richardson. He must have been on holidays. He didn't recognize me.

Hey, look after my gun for me, and tell Sam I'm sorry I didn't talk to him before I went.

WELL ADIOS AMIGO,
FROM PARADISE,
MARLO.

I put the fifty-dollar note in my pocket and thought of old Marlo slinking around the Gold Coast. Maybe he would get a job and buy a car. Maybe a film producer would discover him for rotten parts in crime movies. I remembered him and Joseph and me laughing under the lamp post that night we went to Kings Cross. That was one time I didn't think of Marlo as being alone.

21

The ambulance stopped out the front of the cottage without
its flashing lights on. Mrs Freeman was sick so there were no
lessons. Stephanie was being admitted to hospital by her own
choice because Sam said she could die if she kept throwing up.
Angela and I walked out to the ambulance with her while Sam
signed papers for the driver.

Stephanie told us that at the hospital they keep weighing
you all the time to see if you're gaining weight. If you didn't
put on weight they would keep you nailed to your bed.
Stephanie said she didn't want to die, or even to leave the
cottage. She wouldn't be allowed to have visitors for a couple
of weeks.

I noticed Angela was holding onto my arm again as she
was staring at Stephanie. She was white and scared looking.
Stephanie must have noticed, and she said, "It's okay,
Angela, I'm not worried. You and Harris can come and visit
me as soon as you're allowed and bring me a box of chocolates." The ambulance driver came out and put Stephanie in
the back, lying down. "Soft centres," she called out and
waved to us.

Angela, with her grip still on my arm dragged me up the
stairs, sort of urgently. If it was anyone else but soft little
Angela, I would have been seriously worried. She took me
into her room, which looked exactly like mine, only without
the picture. She pulled out her writing pad and wrote, "Sit
down, please Harris". I did. Then she wrote, "My mother is
going to take me home and I want to tell you some things
first."

"Couldn't you tell Sam?" I asked.

"No," she wrote, "I cannot, but you can."

"I don't think I'm a very good person to tell things to,
Angela."

She wrote, "My mother is going to take me home and I have decided to tell you everything."

You know, once I would have really enjoyed Angela telling me all the stuff about herself, but at that moment I felt like I was drowning in other people's lives. I got out my bolt anyway and watched Angela produce about a dozen sheets of paper full of her spidery writing. She looked very tense and anxious.

This is a rough idea of what she wrote:

When she was ten, her real father left home with someone else. He wasn't so nice anyway, so it was no big loss. Two years later her mother married again to this guy called Lewis Oates. He's a really nice guy, and Angela gets along with him great. One night this Lewis character comes into Angela's bedroom. Angela's mother has gone out with her best friend to see this show that Lewis wouldn't go to. He just has on this blue singlet and white underpants. He's drinking from a can of beer, and he sits down on Angela's bed and starts talking to her. She thinks at first this is real nice, even when he starts tickling her. They laugh and fool around for a while. Then he gets into bed with Angela. Angela knows this isn't right but she doesn't say anything. She really likes this Lewis Oates and she wants him to like her. He starts running his hands over her body and between her legs. She tells him to stop it, but he doesn't. He gets her to feel his erection. Then before she can do anything else, he's on top of her. Angela is a bit frightened and she doesn't like the weight of him squashing into her ribs and the smell of his breath. All the air goes out of her lungs when he presses down on her and kisses her with his tongue going into her mouth, because she has to gasp for air. She feels his erection come up between her legs. The pain is like a time she got hit in the eye with a squash ball, only this time she can't scream. What she does is, she bites his lip as hard as she can and he yells out loud and gets off her. He is standing over the bed when Angela's little sister, Cathy, comes in and asks what's wrong. Angela says, "Nothing," and gets Cathy to sleep with her the rest of the night.

About a month later when Angela's mother is out again, he comes into her bedroom to do it again, only this time he forces her onto her face, twisting her arm up behind her back and entering her from behind. The pain is worse than before and he keeps pumping up and down for a long time. She can't yell out because her face is hard into the pillow.

After that he used to sneak into Angela's room when her mother was asleep. He would tell Angela not to make a noise or any trouble or her mother would find out what they had been doing. For some crazy reason Angela said she felt guilty. The thought of telling her mother was too shameful and embarrassing. When she was fourteen, she got pregnant. Her mother refused to hear a word about how she got pregnant — she kept saying you young people haven't got any sense. Her mother got her an abortion, and a supply of the pill.

At this point in Angela's story, I had really had enough. Hearing this kind of stuff sort of makes me feel all tight, like getting pumped up with gas or something. I remember hearing about these drunk guys at a bucks' party once who held the groom-to-be down at a petrol station, and shoved an air hose down his mouth for a joke. It sort of blew him to bits inside — his lungs and stuff. I used to think about that guy trying to stop his mates doing that.

I knew Angela's story wasn't going to stop. I hadn't read why she quit talking. This is why:

One morning she woke up earlier than usual. She was feeling pretty good because Lewis hadn't been into her bedroom for a couple of weeks. She thought maybe he wouldn't come back again. She realised then what woke her up was Cathy, her little sister, crying in the room next to hers. She got up half-asleep and went into Cathy's room. What she saw was Lewis on top of her little sister. Angela screamed or yelled something so loud and hard that she ripped something in her voice box. Lewis got off Cathy, and then her mother came and there was this big scene where Angela's mother tried to stab Lewis with a bread knife, but it was too bendy and it only ended up cutting him a bit. When it all calmed down Lewis stayed away for a few nights and then came back. Cathy went to stay at her grandmother's place, and Angela had stopped talking even though there was nothing they could find wrong with her throat.

What seemed to stick with Angela was that her mother sort of inferred that Angela and Cathy had somehow provoked Lewis to do what he did to them. Angela thinks her mother really likes Lewis a lot. The morning that Angela screamed, and afterwards, no-one ever talked about what happened at all. Angela came to the cottage about three weeks later.

Listening to, or rather, reading Angela, my tired feeling that I hadn't had for a long time started to come back.

"My mother is going to take me home," Angela wrote again. She was crying.

"Why?" I asked.

"Because she said the neighbours think that something is queer about her and Lewis because her two daughters aren't living at home."

"There *is* something queer about her and Lewis."

"I can't go back, Harris, I can't go back. My mother is going to get Cathy back too."

"You'll have to tell Sam, Angela. What can I do?"

"You tell Sam, Harris," she wrote in capitals.

Nobody was holding me down with an air hose in my mouth but that's how I felt.

I told Sam. Sam straight away phoned Youth and Community Services and got on to the district officer-in-charge. This is what I heard him say on the phone.

Do you have a file on Angela Clarke? Yes thank you, I'll wait. Yes that's correct. Yes. Were allegations of sexual assault by a stepfather ever investigated? Yes I'll wait. (*Silence*) Yes. Was she examined by a doctor? Why not? No real evidence, no permission by either parent. I'm not surprised he didn't give his permission ... I know she was pregnant. Did it occur to you that the father might have been her stepfather? The file says the father was a school friend of Angela's? Who reported that? Mrs Clarke. Are you aware that the two children may be taken back to that place?

The conversation went on for some time and I guess I was falling asleep.

Inside my head the blue and green checked
girl was crying my name over and over; Harris
Harris, Harris. The lady with her was lifting
her up, but her fingers were caught
with mine in the chain-wire fence.
She wouldn't let go.

22

When Sharlene's telephone call came through, I was trying to teach Joseph how to play chess. I was beginning to understand just what a feat Mrs Mac had accomplished — teaching me, that is. Joseph couldn't get past the idea of taking pieces rather than using a strategy. That's what took me ages to grasp; to give up easy, small wins and play for a long-term victory. If I was a pawn on the chessboard of life, then Joseph was a draught. I figured Joseph would never quite be playing the same game as everybody else. Anyway I was real pleased to hear that Sharlene was on the phone.

"Harris, is that you?" she asked.

"Hullo, Sharlene. Yes, it's me."

"I didn't know you weren't at home until the other day when I rang your parents. They didn't tell me before. How are you?"

"I'm good, Sharlene. How are you?"

"Oh great. How are Lyndsay and Jacquiline?"

"Terrific. They haven't got much furniture yet but the carpet's paid for and Jacquiline's going to be pregnant."

Sharlene laughed, "I suppose she's going to be 'Mother of the Year' in the *Dentist's Annual*." Old Sharlene's always good for a laugh.

"Have you got a job?" I asked.

"Four nights a week in a bottle shop just around the corner. It's okay."

"Are you in that squat at Darlinghurst?"

"Yeah. There's no phone so you can't call."

"What's your address? I can write to you."

"168 Charles Street."

I wrote it down and Sharlene went quiet for a while. "I found out where my mother is living the other day," she said.

"Aunty Kathleen?"

"I got the phone number and rang her up. She said she was sorry about leaving and all that. She even cried a bit. She said I could come and live with her as soon as she moves into her new house. She's on the waiting list for a Housing Commission place."

"That's good," I said.

"Hey, Harris, you haven't got any money, have you?"

I remembered Marlo's ticket money. "Fifty dollars," I said.

"No, it doesn't matter. I need more than that."

"I could borrow some."

"No, don't worry, I just thought ... no, it doesn't matter."

"I can send you some."

"No, don't worry, I get paid in a few days." There was a long pause, then she said very softly, "What happened to you, Harris?"

It sort of caught me off guard. I felt a bit like crying and getting sick and getting angry all at once. Since I'd been at the cottage I had been able to keep Clementine right out of my mind. Sharlene just asks me softly, what happened, and there's Clementine. Jammed in the bottom of that refrigerator, and the smell of shit and the colour of her face and the coldness of her skin. And that scream of Helen's.

I must have hung up on Sharlene, I don't remember. Sam was waiting for me in his therapy room.

We sat in the big old lounge chairs. Sam, for once, looked tired. You never expect people like Sam to look tired. They're always asking everyone else how they feel so that you assume they must feel great themselves to be able to keep asking all the time.

"You look tired," I said.

"I am, Harris."

"You worried about Angela?"

"And Stephanie, and Marlo, and Joseph, and you." Sam rubbed his face. "And the whole cottage program."

"You want a cup of tea?" I asked.

"Do you have coffee?" Sam mimicked me and laughed his good laugh. "Jesus, Harris, for the first time since I started this program I feel like it's failing." He rubbed his face again. "Look at Marlo, he's run off to Queensland, Stephanie's lost so much weight she's had to go to hospital, and Angela is being taken back to ... that ... her ... home. And she still doesn't talk."

I got Sam his cup of coffee and we both sat there sipping and thinking. I consider myself as a kind of specialist in failure, and I wondered about Marlo and Stephanie and Angela and Sam. I think sometimes you think you fail at something, when in fact what happens is, you just didn't hit the target you aimed at. What might be the real problem is getting the right target in the first place. I remember when I used to throw that tomato stake around in our backyard, when I wanted to get my picture in the glass case at school. I didn't so much fail as a javelin thrower, I guess I failed when I aimed to be the kid in the glass case. What did happen though; I got this powerful right arm and I used to be able to toss a ball around real hard. After a tomato stake, a ball is a piece of cake.

I said to Sam, "Maybe before Marlo came here, if that stuff happened with Fish-head, he might have really killed him first and then run away. And Stephanie; when I first came here she didn't seem like she wanted to stay alive, but she does now. And Angela wants to stop what's happening at home instead of putting up with it."

"Jesus, Harris, who's the counsellor here?" Sam laughed. Sam knew what I meant though. Not everyone can throw javelins (or even tomato stakes), and not everyone gets their picture in a glass case.

Sam asked me about Mrs Mac. I had hardly talked to Sam about her. I told him how I used to mow her lawns and how she helped me pass the Ranger exams, and stuff like that. I told him about Julius and about Frank and about her bookshop and her weird food.

We sat quietly for a long time.

"Your mother told me she had to drag you screaming to school when you first started kindergarten."

"Yeah, well I was very perceptive, even then."

Sam laughed. "You even got sick, and wouldn't eat at school. Have you never liked school?"

"I don't think so." I told Sam about Miss Imperago and her saying I was retarded and how my parents went funny about it.

We sat quietly again.

"Who is Clementine?"

"What?"

"Clementine. You say that name in your sleep quite regularly."

"I don't know," I say to Sam. But I do know. We don't say anything for a while. Sam lets me just sit there. I don't stop Clementine from coming through.

This time I see Clementine grabbing hold of my leg and calling me Hazz; sitting in my lap and making me do "round and round the garden" on her toes a million times and giggling her head off; me chasing her through the house and hearing her high-pitched squeal, and finding the hidden people in her scummy old book. I see her mother's dark hair and flashing brown eyes.

I tell Sam that Clementine is a little kid I used to know.

23

One time when I was little I must have heard about souls. Probably in church. I used to imagine these things like silver bicycle pumps with the handles drawn out and flattened by a steamroller. They would sort of glide up towards heaven. These were souls. They were always doing it at night for some unknown reason — the gliding upwards, that is. I think I must have heard about lonely souls, and poor souls, and old souls — so there they were, very isolated, flattened, silver pumps in the night.

When I was even littler, I used to lie in bed late at night and hear the whistle of the old steam engines they don't run anymore. I used to think at night the trains came through our house and up the hallway. It's incredible just how dumb you can be when you're little and you put different facts together the wrong way. I don't tell anyone that kind of stuff because I imagine they would think I was crazy even from way back then.

When I was in fourth grade I used to play marbles a real lot. There was this kid called Billy Channell who used to play a lot too. Billy Channell and me were the best marble players in the school. We never played against each other until one day there was no-one left who would play either of us. I had a pillowcase at home half full of starries, and bottlers, with a few steelies and clay-dabs. Billy Channell had more than I had, but he used to buy a lot of his rather than just win them. I always felt sort of a bit purer than him, because I never bought any, but when you think of it, it's probably worse to beat other kids and take theirs. Anyway this Friday Billy and I arranged to get to school early, just the two of us, to have a game of "big-ring". At school we had this place between a fat gum-tree and a peppercorn tree where the grass had been squashed away by kids' feet, and the ground was like my mother's face powder. Unless you could fire really hard, your marble would plop dead in the dust. Billy and I could both fire really hard. We put four in the ring each and he went first. One of the differences between Billy and me was that Billy was good at just about every sport and I was only good at marbles. He was a left-hander and he held the marble sort of cradled in the first joint of his pointer, while I held mine on the top. He used to squat while I got on my knees. It didn't matter about your knees, except they went this sort of varnish colour which you could hardly wash off. Anyway we played three games and he had four of mine and I had four of his (bought ones). An audience started gathering. The little kids got in the front, then the kids from our class. You could tell they were taking sides. I think a lot of problems could be avoided if people didn't always have to take sides. A lot of kids seemed to be on my side, which made me real nervous and my hand started shaking and I noticed it getting a lot dirtier because I was probably sweating. Billy was three up on me, and some of my supporters were shaking their heads. There were girls there too; I remember I never looked at them directly but I was very conscious of them.

Well, this is what happened. We only had time for one more game before the bell. We put five in each, and I went first. I remember how everything sort of slowed down, and the other kids' voices sounded like they were coming from down a tunnel. Someone must have been squashing the little hard berries, because I could smell peppercorn at the back of my nostrils; and the little kids were catching cicadas and making them sing that screeching noise by rubbing their fingers along their backs. I fired my best taw and heard it hit square-chit on Channell's starry.

"Shit, he split it in half," someone said.

I fired again and knocked out his second; then his third. No-one was talking. Even the cicadas had shut up. I felt like all the little bits of my body were working together, perfectly. I could dance, sing, fly. I could knock marbles out of the ring all day with a hanky over my eyes. I knocked them all out. The ten of them. One for every year of my life.

24

Mrs Clarke arrived in a taxi. She was a huge woman with big hands and feet. It was hard to think of tiny Angela coming from her. Sam told the taxi driver not to wait and took Mrs Clarke into his office. I could hear some of what they said when I stood in the hall. Sam's voice and then Mrs Clarke's would get loud and sharp every now and then.

She said stuff like, "I could get the district officer down here, if you like," and "What have you done for her — does she talk?" Sam either didn't say anything to this, or he said it too soft for me to hear. "The only mistake I made," Mrs Clarke's voice was high and piercing, "was to let my girls move out of their own home."

Eventually Sam came out, went upstairs and brought Angela down to his office.

"You do want to go home with me, don't you darling?" Mrs Clarke asked Angela. To my astonishment, Angela must have nodded to this. "You see," said Mrs Clarke.

When you think about it, I suppose it's a bit difficult to tell your mother you don't want to go home with her. I remember my mother once asked me to read this essay I wrote for school to a group of her friends from the church. I really didn't want to do it, partly because I was shy and partly because it was a dumb essay about this paint these two kids invented that made things invisible. Even an exhibitionist wouldn't have wanted to read it out loud. Mothers are people you can't say no to very easily. And if ever you can, you feel guilty as hell.

Mrs Clarke had a bit of a cry, like somebody relieved of a worry. Maybe she felt that getting Angela back was turning out easier than she thought. She probably was worried that Angela would say she didn't want to go home with her.

Joseph came up the hall. On Fridays he finished technical college early. "What's happening?" he asked me. I told him. "That's too bad," he said, "I was just getting to like Angela's conversation, ha ha ha ha, Angela's conversation, get it?" I told Joseph I got it, and asked him to shut up because I was listening.

"Shit, there'll only be you and me left here," he said. "I wonder if Sam will get some more kids in. What do you reckon, Harris?" I told him that I reckoned the cottage might close down soon. This seemed to shock him a bit and he left for the kitchen shaking his head.

Mrs Clarke was making leaving noises in Sam's office. Angela came out, went upstairs and came down again carrying a small carry bag. I left the hall and went out the front door to the gate. I wanted to say goodbye to Angela.

I stood in the sun and felt the skin on my scalp get hot. The brightness made me remember this painting of a wheatfield. I think it was painted by Vincent Van Gogh. In one hand Angela had her carry bag, and the other was held by her mother. They stood talking to Sam on the steps of the cottage. Angela stared at her feet. Mrs Clarke said something about coming back later on to get Angela's clothes. Sam did not smile much. He said goodbye to Angela with a hug. My head was aching and I felt tired. A drip of sweat slid down my inside leg. Mrs Clarke and Angela walked up to me and said goodbye. Angela's eyes were red and sore looking. I didn't touch her, as Mrs Clarke opened the gate and they passed through.

I thought that I shouldn't have waited in the sun so long. My head hurt. Mrs Clarke was a very big woman and made Angela look even smaller. Even though I could see only the back of her head, I knew Angela was crying. My fingers tightened on the iron gate. She turned her head around as she was walking away, trying to wave to me. My fingers hurt.

She threw down her bag and wrenched her hand from the lady holding it. My fingers hurt from climbing. She ran back towards me. The lady quickly followed and caught

her at the gate. Her fingers twisted
around mine. Tears ran down her face.
"Harris, Harris, Harriz, Hazz, Hazz, Hazz,"
she cried.

Something pulled me off the gate, as I saw her being taken away by the hand. I ran through the front door of the cottage and up to my room. I ripped open my wardrobe door and felt in the pouch for Marlo's gun. It was there with the bullets still taped to it. I wiped the stickiness from them, and fitted them into the gun. My head was thumping and I could feel my chest hurt with breathing too hard. When I got back to the front gate, they had gone.

The sun was even hotter than before. I put the gun in the pocket of my pants, and held the galvanised bolt tightly in my fist. I looked down the length of the street in both directions. It was empty. Through the kitchen window, I could see Joseph eating something. As I passed through the gateway, the cottage looked grey and empty.

I ran down the street in the direction they disappeared until I was panting for air at a corner bus shelter. Within seconds a Central Station bus stopped and without thinking I got on.

The passengers on the bus stared vacantly out of windows or at the backs of other people's heads. No-one was interested in a puffing boy with a bolt.

At Central Station, I kept reading the indicator boards for some place to go, until I saw "Chamberlain", and that's where I bought a ticket to. I had to break Marlo's fifty dollars to pay for it.

Sitting in the carriage I felt a lot calmer. Trains sort of do that to me. A room full of strangers being jiggled together, I think, is very soothing.

Directly opposite me there was a group of three smart-arse high school kids, two boys and a girl, who looked like they were coming back from playing cricket or tennis or something. Alongside me was a little Italian man and his wife. The biggest boy kept telling the other two dirty jokes and they would all sort of snigger as if the Italians and I were too stupid or too insignificant to worry about. I looked out the window and tried to let the train keep me calm. I tried thinking about Mrs Mac and then Sam and then Sharlene. I imagined how each of them seemed able to control things around them so well.

The big boy opposite was openly pulling faces at me while the other two were killing themselves laughing. He held his index finger up to his ear and crossed his eyes like he was nuts. I realised I had the bolt up to my ear. The Italian man and his wife must have been used to this kind of thing because they pretended they couldn't understand anything of what was going on. I looked straight at the big boy who dared me with his eyes to say anything. He pretended the finger in his ear was a telephone and this really broke the other two up.

I felt the gun in my pocket and imagined what it would be like to hold it against his cheek. Sharlene would have done that; Sam and Helen wouldn't have. Sometimes, I think *not* doing things is harder than doing them.

The train stopped at Chamberlain and I got out. I could see the three high school kids jammed against the window, pulling faces as the train pulled out.

The front door was open so I walked straight in to the living room. My father was watching something on television. He switched the set off when he saw me. He really looked surprised.

"Where is she?" I asked.

"She's in the kitchen," he said. "What are you doing home?" He followed me into the kitchen. He must have thought I meant my mother. She was bent over the sink.

"Harris, what are you doing here?" she said.

"I just asked him that," my father said.

"Are you supposed to be out?" my mother asked.

"Where is she?" I said.

"Where is who?" she answered.

"The blue and green checked girl."

"What on earth are you talking about?"

"You took her away."

"Who? Who are you talking about?"

"The girl in the blue and green checks."

"You're not making sense, dear."

"You pulled me off the fence, you wouldn't let me go."

"Sit down, I'll make you a cup of tea."

"You're not well, son," said my father.

"That woman took her away . . . she was going to school . . . and the lady took her away . . . you wouldn't help me get her back . . . "

"I'm going to call the doctor," my father said.

I must have pulled the gun out instead of the bolt because both my parents got very frightened looking.

"All right, son, I won't call the doctor, just sit down and your mother will make a cup of tea." My father looked at my mother. "Would you put that gun away?" he said to me.

His lips went into a tight straight line and his face was white. My mother had tears in her eyes. We sat just looking at each other for a really long time, like three very tired people. My headache eased off and my mother made a cup of tea and everything began to feel like it used to — before I started being crazy.

I thought about my parents — living together for thirty years. I wondered what it was that made me feel there was something wrong with them. Maybe it was my craziness. And then I thought that maybe when some people stay close together for a long time, like married for ten or twenty years or something, they imprison each other. What might happen is that people like that won't let the other one be anything more than what they have already got used to. Like if one of them after twenty years says something like, "Penelope, I want to go live on a desert island," or something, and he's been an accountant for a hundred years, then Penelope will say something like, "Don't be silly, George, you know you get sunburnt and hate sandflies." Like if she didn't know about his sunburn and sandflies — if he was a stranger — Penelope might be pretty interested in George. But George is all sealed up in Penelope's head and George can't ever get out. Not as far as Penelope's concerned. The thing about some people like my parents is, they won't let other people change.

Even sitting quietly with my parents sipping tea, I knew I couldn't keep the blue and green checked girl out any longer. I remember at the movies once there was this horror picture which had this bedroom in it where two opposite walls would slowly roll inwards to squash the victims flat. That was sort of like the feeling I had — that it was inevitable, no matter how much you tried to hold it back.

"Who is she?" I asked my father.

"I don't know who you mean," he answered.

"The little girl in the blue and green checked uniform." He looked at my mother.

"Do you know what he's talking about?"

You could hear the cars whooshing by on the road in front of the house. There was a hollow in the road just near the driveway which made every car's tyres go thump, thump, as they passed. A tear rolled down my mother's nose.

"We both know who he's talking about," my mother said.

They looked at each other real hard like people look at old photographs they haven't taken out for a long time.

"I don't want that talked about," my father said to my mother.

She began these big sobs and covered her face with her hands.

"See that," he said to me, "that's why I don't want it talked about. Look what it does to your mother." His face was white. "There are lots of things that are best left forgotten ..."

"I haven't forgotten," my mother cried.

"Some things just cause upset and pain."

"I haven't forgotten her," my mother said again.

"I have," my father said angrily. "I have forgotten it. It had to be you," he turned to me, "you, to bring it all up, to cause all the pain." He got to his feet. "Look what you're doing to your mother. Go away. Go away. Go back to your cottage."

"Who is she?" I yelled very loud.

My father turned on me. "She was your sister," he shouted. "Now get out!"

"What is her name?" I asked my mother.

"Christine," my mother cried. "You used to call her Chrissie." My father looked as if he would hit me.

"What happened to her?" I asked very quietly.

"She was taken away," my mother sobbed through her fingers. My father had his hands over his ears. I felt very odd, sort of queasy and dizzy. I must have asked why she was taken away.

"Because she wasn't ours. Six years we had her, and she wasn't ours. Her real mother came and took her back."

I said the name Chrissie to myself; "Chrissie."

My father grabbed the front of my shirt and screwed it up into his fists. "Leave us alone," he yelled at me. "She's gone, she's gone. It should have been you, not her."

"Don't say that," my mother said.

"I loved her," he said.

"We all did," my mother answered. "Harris, too."

"We should have tried to get her back," my father said.

"We did try."

"Not enough. We didn't try enough, we should have gone to court."

"We couldn't afford it, then, you know that, and we wouldn't have won."

"We might have, we might have won. I should have mortgaged the house. She didn't want to go. She couldn't even understand what was happening. I never should have taken her into our home in the first place. I never should have done it." My father was sort of kneeling at my mother's feet as she sat. He sounded different to any time I could ever remember him.

I walked out the front door without either of them noticing. It was cooler outside and getting dark. I could hear an electric train on the tracks in the distance. I began walking without thinking for some time before I realised I was entering Greening Hills. I walked past Mrs Htsu's place and noticed her lawn edges weren't done very well. I found Lyndsay and Jacquiline's house at the end of a cul-de-sac. It looked small and neat and like all the other houses.

25

Jacquiline answered the door. She had on a dressing-gown and something on her face that looked like porridge.

"Harris, what are you doing here?" she said. "Come in. My mother's here tonight."

"Is Lyndsay home?" I asked.

"No, he's away for three days. He's gone to Melbourne with his boss. Lyndsay's doing very well. I'm sorry we had that argument, Harris."

Jacquiline's mother had her feet up on the lounge and a glass of something in her hand. "Hullo, Harris," she said. "You've been sick, I hear. How are you now, darling?"

"Hullo, Mrs Linquist," I said. "I'm fine, thank you."

"You don't look too well, dear. Come and sit next to me." She swung her feet off the lounge.

"You still at the Pizza Hut, Mrs Linquist?"

"Oh yes, still running around in my little red and white uniform with the Pepsi hat. Oh, yes, still at the Pizza Hut." Jacquiline's mother was pretty drunk.

"Would you like a cup of coffee, Harris?" Jacquiline asked. "No, you drink tea, don't you?"

"Thanks, Jacquiline," I said. She went out to the kitchen.

"I think I'm going to die in that Pizza Hut. One day I'm just going to flop over into someone's Hawaiian thick crust. Do you know what, Harris? I'll bet when I do, the whole place will go on poking pizza down their necks. In fact, probably the one who gets my face in his Pizza will demand a free one, and a fresh tablecloth." She gave a rough cackle at this thought which sounded like Lucille Ball's raspy laugh. Jacquiline came back.

"Would you like to see the house?" she asked me. I followed her into the kitchen where she started pulling out drawers and cupboards and switching on electrical stuff. I said it looked very nice. The bedroom and bathroom were small and tidy. Jacquiline got very excited and saved the baby's room up till last. "Close your eyes," she said. She pulled me by the hand into the room. "Now open them." The room looked very nice if you like babies' things and pink and white and lace and stuff.

"It's beautiful, Jacquiline," I lied.

"Do you think so, Harris? I did it all myself."

"It's really beautiful, Jacquiline." I felt very tired and my head had started aching again.

"I'm so glad you like it."

"I wanted to ask Lyndsay something," I said to Jacquiline.

"He'll be back in three days."

"I wanted to ask him about our sister."

"What are you talking about? You haven't got a sister."

"We had a sister, but she was taken away."

"Come and have a cup of tea."

Back in the lounge room, Jacquiline's mother was stretched out on the lounge again. "I miss him, you know, Jacq," she said.

"I think you should have some coffee," Jacquiline said. She went out to the kitchen.

"I miss him in bed at night. That's when I miss him," she said. "Ten years. You wouldn't think you would remember so clearly, would you? He was only a little man but he was very energetic. We used to cuddle up in bed in winter and talk under the blankets. You never knew him, did you, Harris? Lovely man. It's not the sex. I do miss the sex, but it's the cuddles and the talking under the blankets I miss."

I excused myself and went to the toilet. Even with my head pounding and the confusion about my sister, I was careful as always to pee so that it didn't make any noise that anyone could hear. I can't stand it when people can hear me going to the toilet. The best way is to pee on the porcelain on the side just before the edge of the little water pool in the bowl.

Jacquiline had my cup of tea resting on a cork place mat

with Prince Charles's face on it. "Would you like to see the wedding photos?" she asked me.

"He would have loved your wedding," Mrs Linquist said.

"Harris was there, mother. Drink your coffee."

"Not Harris, your father. Your father would have made a wonderful speech and he would have looked so handsome."

"And you both could have got drunk."

"That's not very nice, Jacquiline," she said. Jacquiline opened a large album on my lap. There were hundreds of photographs of relatives and Lyndsay and Jacquiline.

"Our wedding was in a registry office. We didn't have a penny. Not like you lot today, getting it all on a plate. Your father wasn't one for wasting money."

"Not having any helped a lot," said Jacquiline.

"You see how cruel she can be, Harris, after all I've done for her."

I could see that maybe Jacquiline wasn't so much of a pain as I thought. That Mrs Linquist, even if she gave free Pepsis, was a pain in the arse. She was probably one of those people who is very generous and kind and patient to strangers and workmates and customers, but didn't work too hard at it with her own family.

I told Jacquiline I was sorry about the wedding reception I ruined and that I thought that Lyndsay in fact was a really lucky guy, and that I didn't think she had too many teeth. She got real happy then and hugged me. I promised to design this fabulous garden for her when I felt better.

I said goodbye to Mrs Linquist and Jacquiline and went out into a starry night.

Within about five minutes of walking along the street, I got this idea of going to Chamberlain High School. I don't know why, I just wanted to see inside the place.

Some of the lights were on in the school buildings. I climbed over the fence. The principal's office was partly lit and I couldn't resist cupping my hands between the glass and my face to see better. Inside there was the old glass case with the photograph of the javelin champion kid. I felt the concrete grooves of the building and remembered Miss Imperago and her big tits, and her telling my mother I was backward.

Along the verandah was the classroom I spent the most time in. I could see shadowy shapes of furniture inside faintly lit from an outside fluorescent light. My old desk was hidden in the shadows. I took my shoe off and cracked a window pane. Some glass fell inwards as I reached in, opened the lock and forced the window upwards. I felt the broken edges slice my hand. Inside there were stale school smells of chalk and dust and paper. I moved to the back of the room and sat at my old desk, pressing my bleeding hand against the front of my shirt.

Most times Billy Channell used to sit alongside me. The closest girl was Marie Demeril. I used to do ballroom dancing with Marie. Our bodies used to fit together perfectly when we danced. They touched from the knees to the shoulders like two big S's clipped together. We did this tango, and the dancing teacher taught us some extra steps — because we looked good together, I think. Once, the other kids stopped dancing and watched us. I deliberately got this bored-looking expression on my face and talked to Marie to make everyone think I could tango in my sleep. Marie told me her father was being transferred to Wilcannia. I asked where Wilcannia was; it was about six hundred miles west. We did the tricky new bit and a few kids clapped. Marie and I only ever danced together, we never did anything else. I asked was she going to Wilcannia too. She was. The record-player was playing "Fernando's Hideaway". When the music stopped, she leaned her face very close to my ear and whispered, "I'll miss you."

After a while I stopped doing ballroom dancing. It never seemed the same without Marie. She certainly could dance. I always sort of suspected that it was really her that led me through all the difficult bits. Sometimes you get people like that — like Marie — who will let you feel good about something that they are mostly doing.

I could see old Buggawhite up near the blackboard, pandering to the girls.

Outside in the playground I could hear hundreds of kids running and yelling, trying to stop the time running out and the bell ringing to drag them back into their cells. I remember this red ants' nest Lyndsay and I found at the cemetery once. They kept running in and out of their holes with bits of food and other dead ants and stuff. We made up this sort of poison from old bottles of medicine and paint, and we used to pour it on the ant hills. The ants would run around really fast, in and out of their holes, in and out; like as if they could stop it happening if only they ran fast enough, or something.

I wondered where they all were, right at that moment; Marie, Billy Channell, old Buggawhite, Miss Imperago, and all the kids in the class. People just disappear really. One day you realise that you haven't seen them for a long time — but you never remember saying goodbye to them or anything. You think you'll always see everyone at least one more time.

On the underside of my desk, I felt around for the H. B. I once carved in it with my biro. It was still there alongside this wonky map of Australia. It wasn't easy carving a map of Australia upside down. Once I got under the desk to look at it. That's how come I know it's wonky.

I sat on the teacher's desk, with the bolt in my hand, and said goodbye to the old classroom and to the other kids and to Marie and Billy, and even old Buggawhite. You probably shouldn't go back to old places you used to know real well — because they make you feel like you just missed a bus or a train or something.

26

On the train back to the city, the carriage I was in was mostly empty. I had decided to see Sharlene to ask her about my sister. I stared out the window trying to remember the address she had given me. When I had given up trying, it just came to me: 168 Charles Street. Remembering is often like that, like it's got its own clock which isn't concerned with when you want the memory back. I thought of this giant memory filing system of shelves stretching out of sight and these little people running around trying to get your bit of information out of storage when you want it. I imagined the cursing and swearing about stuff being put in the wrong places and stuff being covered up and some being hidden and others lost. And them being out to lunch when a request comes in. Life in the old memory system wouldn't be all that relaxing. If you kept thinking stuff like that all the time — I figured you would be totally crazy instead of half crazy.

The taxi let me out in front of a row of semi-detached houses which looked identical. They looked like those ones you see in movies about old Welsh mining-towns where the houses have names on little plates on the front, like TWYCHRYBLETHN or something.

I knocked at the front door and Sharlene opened it.

"Harris, what are you doing here? Come in. You've got blood on your shirt."

"I cut my hand on some glass."

"Let me have a look." Sharlene looked at my hand and got a bandaid for the cut. The house was tiny, and the furniture looked like it came from the tip. Even so, it was sort of cosy, and there were a lot of stained-looking cushions on the floor.

"Where's Kaylene?" I asked.

"Kaylene? Oh, she left months ago."

"Do you know anything about my sister?"

"What sister?"

"Her name's Christine."

"You haven't got a sister, Harris. Are you all right?"

"They told me at home. I used to have a sister called Christine and she was taken away when I was little."

"I never heard of her, Harris."

The front door opened then, and in came this twenty-year-old guy, with a guitar and tattooed dotted lines on his wrists with the words "cut along dotted lines" on them. Most of his hair had been shaved off and he looked yellow and unhealthy. "Who's this?" he said to Sharlene.

"My cousin, Harris. Harris, this is Steven."

"You've got blood on your shirt," he said. "Hey, listen to our new number." He got this real serious look on his face, strummed his guitar and sang this song about the desert in the city, and the rain in the sewer filling waterbeds of pain, or something like that.

"What do you think?" he asked. "Stafford's going to get his mate to make a video clip for us."

"Have you got any money, cous?" he asked me.

I pulled out what was left of Marlo's money. "About forty dollars," I said.

"Wo ho!" Steve jumped up. "Just the right amount for our forty-dollar package." He ran off to a back room and came back with a brown paper bag. "How about these?" he said as he passed me some black and white photographs. The photos had a whole lot of naked people twisted together. "I've got better ones — kids, animal, torture. See this one. I got five dollars up the Cross for this one."

Sharlene reached over and snatched the photographs off both of us. "He doesn't want them," she said.

"How do you know?" He leant over to me and said, "You want to see some of the really hard stuff? Forty-dollar stuff?"

"No thank you," I said.

"You a fag?"

"Shut up, Steven, he's my cousin."

"That doesn't mean he ain't queer."

"Sing us your song again," Sharlene said.

"Get stuffed. Hey, how about a forty-dollar investment in my musical career, cous?"

"He needs his money, Steven," Sharlene said.

"So do I. I gotta walk around for two hours to sell five stinkin' bucks worth."

"For Christ's sake, Steven!"

"I've got to go anyway, Sharlene," I said.

"No, don't go yet," said Steven, pushing my shoulder down and forcing me to sit. "Let's have a drink." To Sharlene he said, "We have got something to drink, haven't we?"

"Yes. Would you like a drink, Harris? A Coke?"

"Yes, thanks," I said.

"What are you into, cous?" Steven asked me.

"Harris has been away on a sort of holiday, haven't you, Harris?"

"Yes," I answered.

"A holiday? I haven't had a holiday since ... since ... Shit, I never had a holiday." He strummed a chord on his guitar, and sang, "I ain't had no holiday (strum), Since I was just a kid (strum), I ain't had no holiday to rest my tired bones in (strum)." Sharlene brought the drinks in. "Where've you been on holiday, cous?" he asked.

Sharlene answered, "In Glebe."

"Glebe? What sort of holiday is that?"

"Actually Harris hasn't been well. He's been convalescing in a nursing home."

"You haven't got any diseases, cous?" he asked, genuinely afraid.

"No," I answered.

"Listen, I've got an idea," he said to Sharlene. "You go and get some take-away fried rice, and the cous here can stay for a while." He gave Sharlene two dollars.

"Harris can't stay," Sharlene said.

"Actually, I've got to go."

"It'll only take fifteen minutes. I'll sing for him."

"Is that okay, Harris?" Sharlene looked tense.

"Yes," I said.

"I won't be long," Sharlene called as she left.

Steven sang another serious song about how everyone was chasing this flying dollar around the place until they all ended up down this giant sinkerator or something. It was even worse than the other one. I felt very tired and my head was hurting again. I stayed because of Sharlene.

"That'll be forty bucks," Steven said to me.

"What for?"

"For the song."

"I'm sorry, but I think I need it."

"Give me the fuckin' money or I'll smash your fuckin' head in." He held his guitar over one shoulder. I could smell his bad breath.

"You'll break your guitar," I said. He thought for a second, drew the guitar back as if he was going to bash me with it. Then he put it down, got up and went to the kitchen drawer and came back with a large carving knife.

"This doesn't break," he said, holding it against my stomach.

"All right," I said. I reached into my pocket and took out Marlo's gun. I put the barrel against his cheek and said, "When the bullet comes out the back of your head, a lot of your brain gets sucked out with it." I just made that up because I thought it would sound very scary.

"Okay, okay. Look ... I'm putting the knife down, okay? ... Okay, kid? See the knife is down. Be careful, will you."

"I've killed two people this week. One was pretty old but the other was about your age. I like to kill people. That's why I'm mostly not allowed out. Put the knife back in the drawer and I won't kill you, because you're Sharlene's friend. I never killed any of Sharlene's friends — yet." I wiped at the blood on my shirt and Steven watched every stroke very carefully. "I don't usually get blood on myself."

When Sharlene returned with the fried rice, we all ate

very quietly. Sharlene kept asking Steven whether there was anything wrong.

I sat in Sharlene's toilet for a long time, hoping my headache would go away. When I came out Steven must have been waiting behind the door because he jumped on my back and I fell to the ground with my arms pinned under me, and Steven on top of me. I could feel his hand go into my pocket, looking for Marlo's gun. I thought this is probably a bit like what being raped is like. I yelled very loud and rolled Steven off my back. He pulled the gun out of my pocket and aimed it at me. The problem for Steven was, he wasn't actually holding Marlo's gun, he was holding my galvanised bolt. I got the gun out of my other pocket, aimed it at Steven and pulled the trigger.

Sharlene must have been locked in a bedroom or somewhere because I could hear her thumping on a door and calling out. Steven was all scrunched up in a corner of the room. I picked my bolt up off the floor and saw how he was shivering, with his eyes all squinted. There wasn't any blood coming out of him that I could see. His guitar had a neat round hole in it just near where you strum it. When I was staring at Steven and his guitar, I realised I could have killed him. I didn't know whether I had wanted to kill him or not. I was glad he wasn't lying there with his brains coming out of his head. My headache got worse just then in a big wave from the back of my skull to the front, like as if the bullet had gone through my brain. I got this feeling I was really mad and that maybe I didn't know what I was doing anymore.

I ran out of Sharlene's house towards Chippendale.

27

Mrs Mac's bookshop had different books than before in the window but it looked just as crowded. I could see two customers inside. One was talking to Helen, the other was trying to fit down the aisle. I pushed through the door and waved to her. She waved back, excused herself with the customer and picked her way carefully over to me.

"Hullo Harris." She seemed pleased to see me. "Go through the back door and wait for me inside. I'll be about fifteen minutes or so. Julius is there." I edged towards the back of the shop, picking up the books that plopped to the floor as I brushed past.

In the kitchen, Julius was sitting at the table colouring in a Corn Flakes packet picture of a kangaroo with boxing gloves. I was surprised to see him still up. He looked older than I remembered, and thinner. I said, "Hi." He said nothing. He looked up from his work once and then continued colouring. I sat down opposite him and watched. When most little kids do something like colouring in, they get this concentrated look on their faces and they twist their mouths and tongues around sort of following what they're doing. Julius's face wasn't doing that at all. It was just sort of still and empty.

"What are you doing?" I asked, which was really stupid. He looked at me, then went on colouring in.

"I'm sorry about your father," I said, but I didn't know why I said it.

"You didn't know him," he said without looking up.

"I met him once, at your old place, remember?" Julius held up his kangaroo to me.

"Finished," he said.

" It's very good." He put it down again.

"When is mummy coming ?" he said.

124

"She's nearly finished in there," I said. He got off his chair and found himself a sandwich that Helen must have left for him. "What school do you go to?" I asked.

"It's holidays," he said.

"I know, but what school do you go to when it's not holidays?"

"The one around the corner."

"You like it?"

"Do you want to play?"

"Your mother will be here in a minute."

"Can we play hide 'n' seek?" Actually I didn't feel like playing anything right then. I felt like going to sleep to get away from my headache. I didn't answer Julius. "Can we play hide 'n' seek, Harris?" he asked again.

I'm really a sucker for people when they use my name or look all pitiful or something. I felt sorry for Julius for the second time. "I'm too tired, Julius," I said.

"Just one."

"Okay, just one game."

"You count," he said.

"One, two, three, four, five, six, seven ..." Julius ran off into the back rooms. I kept counting to one hundred and then sang out. "Coming, ready or not." But I wasn't. Coming, that is. I couldn't actually get up out of the chair. I felt a bit sick in the stomach. It wasn't that I was too weak, or anything, but rather that I just sat there knowing I couldn't get up and go look for Julius. For a quick second, I thought to myself, here's where I go really nuts — stuck in a chair for the rest of my life. I scared myself quite a bit. "Julius," I called out, but got no answer. Hiders never answer seekers. I knew that. "Julius, I can't come and get you, I'm too tired to get up. Julius, can you hear me?" I waited in silence for a few minutes, then Julius's head appeared in the doorway.

"You hide me," he said.

"That wouldn't be any good, because I'd know where you were, wouldn't I?" I figured I couldn't be all that crazy.

"Mummy can look for me. You can tell mummy to look for me."

"I don't know this house, Julius."

"Hide me, hide me," he demanded.

"No, I can't."

"Hide me in the 'frigerator."

"What?"

"Like Clementine."

In my head the blue and green checked girl
broke away from the lady holding her hand.
She ran to me and her fingers twisted in
the chain wire. I pulled at the gate.
It swung open. A refrigerator door.
She was cramped in the bottom, her eyes
shut. Her face white. A terrible smell.

"No good wivout Clementine," Julius said. "You shouldna put her in the sink. You shouldna put her in the water in the sink. You did it, Harris, you did it."

"What?" I said.

"You shoulda got hit, not me. I never put her in the sink, you did that. You made her dead, not me." Julius was screaming at me, his face twisted in pain. He tried to punch me, but it didn't hurt much.

I knew Julius's pain. There wasn't anything I could do. I just let his scrunched up fists hit me. I could feel his puffing and panting breath in my face. Eventually he stopped and we just stared at each other. I thought that if Julius had Marlo's gun in his pocket, I'd be dead.

I could hear Helen's old-fashioned cash register pinging in the shop and the sound of muffled voices. I put the bolt to my ear. Julius had his head on the carpet facing up at me. We stayed like that for a long while.

"I lost my sister, too," I said to Julius. "A long time ago. A lady took her away."

Julius was asleep on the floor. Helen was standing in the doorway. For a moment I thought she might scream that horrible scream, but she didn't. She just sat down opposite me and lit a cigarette without saying anything. I went to sleep for a while at that point.

Helen must have made some tea and put Julius to bed while I was dozing. I went to the toilet but nothing happened. We ate some sandwiches in silence. The radio was playing softly and there was a small fan humming on the floor in the corner of the room. I put the bolt back in my pocket. I always got more relaxed and comfortable with Helen.

"Where have you been?" she asked me. I told her the places I had been since I left the cottage — my parents', Jacquiline's, Sharlene's. "Did you cut yourself?" she pointed to the blood on my shirt and the bandaid. I told her of the visit to my old classroom and she smiled and shook her head at me. "You didn't tell me you had a sister," she said. I knew she must have heard me tell Julius, when she was standing in the doorway. I said that I didn't know I had one until tonight — until my mother and father told me. In fact that was what I was doing — trying to find her. I asked Helen if she thought I was crazy. She said, no. But Helen couldn't see inside my head like I could. "Why don't you ring them up and ask them where she is now?" she said. I thought about that for a while and then got on the phone.

"Mum, this is Harris."

"Harris, where are you?" she sounded very tired.

"I'm at a friend's place. I'm okay."

"Your father is very upset."

"I'm sorry."

"It's not really your fault."

"I want to go see her, Mum."

"What did you do with that gun?"

"I gave it back to the person I got it from." My mother remained silent. "I want to see Christine, Mum."

"I don't think your father would want you to."

"I really want to."

"Your father has locked the bedroom door."

"Where does she live, now?"

"I think you should go back to Mr Lehare's cottage and forget this."

"I don't feel real good at the moment. Maybe if I can see her and talk to her or something, maybe I won't feel so bad."

There was a long silence. I could hear my mother's breathing come in long sighed-out breaths.

"You might feel worse after you see her."

"Please, Mum." I could hear her swallow and hold her breath.

"Don't ever tell your father, Harris. He doesn't know that I know where she lives." She gave me the address.

"Are you crying, Mum?"

"No, no, I'm just tired."

"I'll see ya, Mum."

"Goodnight, Harris."

"Goodnight, Mum."

The address she gave me was in East Sydney. Helen asked me to leave it until the next day and she would come with me. I told her I didn't want to wait any longer, and it might be better if I went on my own. She phoned for a taxi.

Before the taxi arrived, I said to Helen, "Julius thinks I . . ."

"I know," she interrupted me.

"We never talked about it."

"We will."

"Maybe Sam could talk to Julius."

"Maybe."

The taxi honked at the front of the shop. I wanted to say something to Helen but I wasn't sure what it could be. She gave me a hug and I hugged her back, and then left through the bookshop.

28

The address was a block of cream brick units. Christine's was number sixteen on the first floor, near the stairway. I knocked and waited. There was no answer. I knocked again. Along the corridor a door opened and a man with red hair, carrying a fat plastic garbage bag, sidled up to me.

"She won't answer," he said. He put the bag down and looked me up and down.

"What do you mean?" I asked.

"Is that blood on your shirt?"

"Yes."

"How did you get that on you?"

"I cut my hand."

"She's not allowed to answer the door to anybody."

"How do you know?"

"I know because I live here, don't I? " I sat down on the steps; the muscles in my legs felt like they had been overstretched.

"She might not be home," I said.

"She's home all right, I know."

"How do you know?"

"Because Mrs Carmine asked my wife to keep an eye on her when she's not around, that's how come I know."

"Who's Mrs Carmine?"

"She's the woman living with her for a while."

"Who else lives with her?"

"No-one at the moment. Except her mother when she's not travelling around somewhere. Who are you?"

"I'm her brother."

"Christine's?"

"Yes."

"She hasn't got a brother, mate."

"She doesn't know about me."

"How can she not know about her own brother?"

"We got separated a long time ago. Who is this Mrs Carmine?"

"She's a social worker friend of her mother's. Big fat bitch. She got my boy into some trouble."

"When does she come?"

"I don't know, she must be out at the moment, because she tells Christine not to open the door to anyone. She won't like you being here, mate, I can tell you."

"I'll wait," I said.

"I know how to get her to answer the door."

"How?"

"That Mrs Carmine has taught her to only open the door for a special knock."

"What?"

"She only opens the door if you knock four times, then wait a second and then knock four times again." I thought that this man might be playing a joke on me; he looked about fifty, with brown blotches on his face. I thought that perhaps this wasn't the right place.

"How old is she?" I asked.

"It's your sister, mate."

"I might be at the wrong place."

"About your age, I'd reckon."

"Why is she minded by this Mrs Carmine?"

"I don't believe for one minute you're her brother, but I couldn't give a stuff, she got my boy into trouble. You'll soon know what's wrong with her when you talk to her, mate. You give the four knocks and four more, you'll soon find out why she's got to be looked after." He gave a snigger, then a loud laugh and carried his garbage bag off down the stairs.

I wondered if I should wait for Mrs Carmine. I could hear the red-haired man talking to someone on the floor below. I stood up and knocked four times waited and knocked four times again. I could hear someone on the other side. The door opened.

"I thought you were Mrs Carmine."

"Christine?"

"Yes."

"I'm Harris."

"Mrs Carmine said I wasn't to talk to any more boys."

"I'm Harris Berne."

"I don't know anything about that. My mother and father have gone to Queensland for a holiday."

"I'm your brother."

"Mrs Carmine said ..."

"Mrs Carmine said it would be okay for me to come in when she told me about the four knocks on the door."

"All right, you can come in, then."

We sat on an expensive-looking lounge in a large room full of paintings and thick carpet and lamps. Christine looked different from what I had imagined. Maybe I still expected this little kid in a blue and green checked uniform or something, I don't know. I didn't feel good at all. My head was buzzing and I still wanted to go to the toilet.

"I've got a job," Christine said. "I'm a sorter. Have you got a job? I sort electrical parts out and Frank puts them in packets. Frank is my friend. He works at the same place as me but he's not a sorter. I don't know you. The boy next door, he's got red hair, and he came in once like you just did, and he told me to take my pants off but Mrs Carmine said not to and not to let boys in anymore. I'm not taking my pants off and you shouldn't be in here. I haven't got a brother. What do you want?"

"Where's the toilet?" I said.

"It's in there." She pointed down a hallway. I found the toilet and vomited all over the floor. The smell was terrible except that I felt a hell of a lot better. I pulled huge lengths of toilet paper off the roll and mopped at the sickly mess on my hands and knees. I dropped the sodden bits into the bowl. The roll of paper disappeared and the floor looked not too bad as I sat on the edge of the toilet seat and wiped at the sweat on my face.

"Are you coming out?" Christine called from outside the door. I opened the door and bumped into her. "What's that smell? You got sick. Mrs Carmine will get you."

"Could I have a glass of water?" I asked.

At that point there were four knocks on the door then four more. "That's Mrs Carmine." Christine opened the front door to a short and very fat lady with a square leather case.

"Who are you?" she said to me.

"Harris Berne," I replied.

"What are you doing here?" She turned to Christine. "I told you never to let anyone in except me."

"He knocked the same as you."

"Did you?" she said to me.

"Yes."

"How did you know what to knock?"

"The man next door showed me."

"With red hair?"

"Yes."

"He's not my brother, is he?" Christine said.

"Your what?"

"He said he was my brother."

"You haven't got a brother," Mrs Carmine said.

"He got sick in the toilet and it all stinks." Mrs Carmine strode into the toilet and came back with a tissue held to her nose.

"You filthy person," she said. "I want you to leave right away."

"And he wanted me to get him a drink," Christine said. "And he wanted me to take my pants off."

"You filthy thing," Mrs Carmine said to me.

"I didn't ..."

"Don't you open your mouth to me, you animal, you, you, filthy ... What were you going to do with her, you horrible boy? Not so brave now, eh, now I'm here. Not so brave as when you've got a defenceless girl alone."

"I didn't say anything about her pants," I said.

"He did, he did, he said rude things to me about my bottom and ... and things like that."

"I'm going to call the police, and you, you can just sit

there." Mrs Carmine picked up the telephone and began dialling.

I felt incredibly tired. My skull felt like it was being pounded by a bag full of sand from the inside. I was angry with this Mrs Carmine and Christine. Being angry felt better. I stood up, grabbed the telephone cable and tore it out of the wall. Mrs Carmine screamed, which made Christine scream. I pulled out the bolt or the gun, I didn't care which, and yelled at them both to sit on the lounge. When I yanked the telephone cable, I must have pulled the bandaid off my cut and opened it up again. The blood dripped down my arm and onto the carpet.

Christine gave a sickening howl and pointed at the blood with her eyes bulging and fell off the lounge to the floor.

"Blood, aaaahh, blood aaahhh, blood," she kept gagging and rocking backwards and forwards on the floor. Mrs Carmine tried to comfort her by putting her arm around her but Christine took her arm and bit hard into the soft flesh near the elbow. Mrs Carmine roared with pain, and Christine started laughing and biting her teeth up and down so that they made a chipping noise. She leapt to her feet still giggling and pulled her pants down, holding her dress up high.

Someone was banging on the front door outside. Mrs Carmine was holding her bitten arm. Christine fell to the floor again and began kicking and thrashing her arms and legs.

Inside my head I watched the blue
and green checked girl and the
lady holding her hand slowly
get smaller and smaller
and finally
disappear
down the
end of
the
street.

29

Cobwebs and splintery bearers and spiders in your hair. In the darkness my fingers scraped against the pounding stone. I groped through the dirt for the hammer. It was gone. There was one piece of stone to be crushed. I decided it was pure white. Actually I had never found a pure white. But it didn't matter when they were wrapped. If no-one ever opened them up — they could all be pure whites.

The underwater sounds of people above me murmured in the boards. I tapped at the stone with the butt of Marlo's gun and it cracked nicely to manageable sizes for the pounding stone. I began work with the old rhythm and the smell of dirt and sweet stone dust.

Above me the voices raised. I stopped pounding with the gun and placed the bolt against the boards.

"You shouldn't have said that to him," my mother said.

"I know, I know. But why couldn't he just leave things as they were?" said my father.

"You don't have to shout at me."

"I'm not shouting at you."

"We should have talked to him about it. Explained it to him," my mother said.

"He was too young."

"I mean later on. We should have explained it all when he was old enough to understand. We've never been open about it. Harris doesn't know what to think ... and I never realised he could remember it from that age."

"Can we just stop this? You're going to have his mental state blamed on us — on me — in a minute. There never was any point in explaining it to him."

"He was very attached to Christine. He didn't care what ... she was like."

"For God's sake, so was I! He was four years old, for Christ's sake. Four years old. What do you think it did to me — still does to me — when we have to go through all this?"

"You could understand it — he couldn't."

"I don't want to talk about it anymore." There was a long silence as someone moved around the room. My mother spoke so softly then that I could just hear her.

"I know about Christine," she said.

"What do you mean?" my father answered.

"I know that Christine was more than a foster child to you. I've always known about her and why you don't want to talk about her. Why you're afraid of Harris."

"What are you talking about? I'm not afraid of Harris."

"I know that Christine isn't the daughter of your brother's friend. She's yours." My mother paused. "And that's why you don't want to talk about it. You're afraid. You've always been afraid that Harris might turn out like her." My mother spoke so quietly and calmly I could barely hear at the end of the bolt.

"When did you know?" my father said, almost as quietly.

"She told me. Christine's mother. Before she took out the court order. She told me if we fought it in court, then the truth would come out and we would all be embarrassed."

"You never said anything."

I took the bolt away from the floorboards. I remembered Sharlene asking me if I ever heard things I wasn't meant to hear — with the bolt, I mean. I knew I had just heard one. I thought about my father having a child with someone else and the child being Christine, and Christine being like she is. Everything seemed out of focus, like when the antenna on the television is in the wrong position.

The gun wasn't as good as the hammer for crushing rock. It took much longer to get to the fine grains. I thought that the metal paint on the gun was probably coming off with every stroke and discolouring the sugar. Above me the telephone rang. I did not want to listen again so I put the bolt in my pocket and continued crushing sugar.

I thought about this time when I must have been about eleven or twelve and we went down the south coast for a two-week holiday near the beach, in a yellow fibro house. Lyndsay and me would get up early, when the tide was out, and we would get pippies. How you get pippies is, you spread your feet on the sand and then you screw backwards and forwards on the balls of your feet until your heels go deep into the sand and you feel a pippy. I never did find "pippy" in the dictionary, but they make good bait anyway. My father taught Lyndsay and me how to do that, and also how to fish off the rocks without getting washed into the surf. I used to wonder who taught him — my father, that is. At lunchtime we used to get so hungry we would eat about a wheelbarrow load of chips and meat pies that burnt your tongue, with sauce and gravy that ran down your arm.

Once we found this old dead eel on the beach that really stank pretty bad. We decided to give mum a bit of a scare for a joke. What we did was, we wound the old eel around and around Lyndsay's neck and propped its mouth open just near his face. We dropped a bit of tomato sauce around Lyndsay's neck, probably a bit too much, and Lyndsay came staggering and lurching into the kitchen with his eyes bulging and his throat croaking for air as if the eel was some kind of snake that had got him. Mum, unfortunately, had just taken a topside roast out of the oven and it went all over the floor and she attacked the eel with this whopping great fork she had in her hand. Lyndsay was the one who almost passed out as he saw the fork coming for his throat. I never forgot that scene. Lyndsay and I never ever knew whether mum was really trying to save Lyndsay's life or whether she played a little joke back on us. I think I was more worried about the roast on the floor, at the time.

I could see a yellow light wiggling towards me. I kept pounding.

"What are you doing?" It was Julius.

"Making sugar."

"That ain't sugar." He shone the torch on the stone. I

recognised my old torch, the one I swapped for the photo album. I wondered if the police light would still flash on the end. I pushed the switch on the handle, but nothing flashed.

"What are you doing here, Julius?"

"Mummy woke me up and said we had to get dressed and come and see you. Can I make some? Can I have something to squash rocks with?"

I got my galvanised bolt out and gave it to him.

"Is all that sugar?" he pointed to the rows of wrapped sugar. "What are you going to do with it all?"

"I don't know," I said.

"I'm going to make lots of sugar," he said.

We both pounded hard for a while.

"Mummy said that she writ a letter and that here it is, and that you can read it to me an' that's why your mummy got the torch, so you can read it to me. But we can still make sugar, can't we?"

Julius kept crushing while I opened Helen's letter. It started with "Dear Harris," in Helen's very even handwriting. I read it out loud while Julius worked. It was hard to read the letter and hold the torch. Helen started writing it a few weeks after Clementine's accident.

Julius stopped crushing with the bolt when I finished reading.

"Do you reckon Clementine felt anything?" he asked me.

"In the refrigerator?"

"Yes."

"No," I said. "You can't feel anything when you're really cold." I just made that up.

"Can't you?" he asked.

"No, you just go to sleep." He started pounding again. I switched the torch off because it was better working in the dark.

"I reckon the 'frigerator did it."

"What?"

"Sent Clementine to sleep."

"I reckon," I said.

Julius and I had synchronised our blows; when I had mine raised, his hit the pounding stone. It went thump, crack, thump, crack, thump, crack, thump, crack. Then a surprising thing happened. I had to switch the torch on to have a good look. Both of us stopped work. The pounding stone had split in half.

After a while I told Julius to go back outside to the others and tell them I'm okay. I shone the torch for him to see his way out.

I started thinking about people I knew; about Marlo, slinking around — an outcast; of Angela injured and sealed off; of Sharlene all crusty and bent. And of Jacquiline trying to please everybody, and Lyndsay and Clementine and Helen and Julius, and my mother and father.

Somewhere along the way when you're a kid you get this idea that everything is supposed to be fair, that your brother shouldn't get more ice-cream than you, that if you wait long enough you get your turn on the swings, that even though he's taller than you — you're faster. And everyone loves this idea when you're a kid, you only have to yell "that's not fair" and someone fixes it up for you. If you think about it, things have to be equal to be fair, and nothing has ever been equal.

I remember my mum telling me about fairness and good and bad luck, and her being superstitious; like spilt salt for sorrow and sugar for joy. I started thinking about superstition and stuff. I mean who's to say there isn't something in it — maybe just some stupid spilt thing happens and everything goes right or wrong.

The beam of the torch focused on the tightly packed bags of sugar stacked at the narrow end of the house. I began counting. The oldest bags, at the back, had sagged over the years and were covered in dust and webs. Each row had taken maybe a year. There were eight rows — thirty or forty bags in a row, each one irregular, each grain hand-crushed.

I wrapped up the last of what Julius and I had made and crawled out of the sugar factory. You have to give up stuff like making sugar sometime.

30

I would like to have been able to say that some astounding event blasted me with light and truth and everything suddenly felt better, but that didn't happen. I think most changes with people happen like drilling teeth — slow and painful.

After I came out I don't remember much of what happened. I know Helen and Sam and my parents were waiting. I think they thought I might shoot myself or something.

I slept for about two weeks at this private hospital that Sam's friend owns, and then spent a few days at Sam's home. At the moment I am living with Helen and Julius — I'll explain about that later.

This is the letter from Helen, that I read to Julius.

DEAR HARRIS,

Feb. 27th: It is four weeks since Clementine's accident. I still can't believe it has happened, I walk into her room because I hear her crying or giggling. I swear I actually hear her, and then when I find the room empty, it all comes back like a terrible nightmare.

Sometimes when I wake up in the morning, the knowledge of what has happened doesn't come crashing through for a minute or so. I can't believe the loneliness and emptiness or the pain. At the funeral I was amazed at how composed and under control I felt. I was able to talk to everyone there. I didn't shed a tear even. It was very unreal, as if it was happening on television, or to somebody else, and it wasn't Clementine, not my Clementine.

Frank has been sick and in hospital. He seems confused and not very coherent. I don't think he would have understood about Clementine, so I didn't tell him.

Do you remember the bruises on Julius's legs? I did that; I was so angry. I explained as best I could to Julius what happened to me. At the hospital I tore the doctor's coat and scratched his face, because he gave up working on her. Can you imagine me doing that?

I was so angry with you, for not watching them properly, I couldn't talk to you. I wanted you to suffer and be in pain and be dead. Then I felt guilty that I had gone out and left them, that it wouldn't have happened if I had been there.

May 6th: I feel so depressed lately, I can't seem to do anything. A lady rang me up three days ago and told me she had read about the accident in the paper and that she had lost her son in a car accident two years ago. It was a help talking to her — she knew what it was like for me. We talked for two hours, and she said the memory is always there but she doesn't find it so painful anymore that she can't get on and do things. I would give anything to have her back, for just a moment, to hold her and show her how much I love her.

July 24th: People have stopped telephoning and dropping in, which I am grateful for. I know they mean to be helpful and considerate, but none of them seems able to talk about Clementine or the accident. I wish you were here so we could talk about it. I don't feel angry with you anymore. There doesn't seem anyone who really knew Clementine all that well, except you and Julius. Julius is very quiet and I don't seem able to help him much. I have tried talking to him but he just closes down and goes away. I have his friends stay over as much as I can, because I know I'm not much company for him.

Aug. 15th: Frank died yesterday. The doctor said he had acute alcoholic liver disease. I wish I hadn't left him. There wasn't much love left, but I think he drank even heavier after we left him. I will have to tell Julius soon. I feel so dreadfully guilty, Harris.

Sept. 3rd: I heard about the cottage you are living in through your cousin, Sharlene. She telephoned and told me. I will come and visit you, but not just yet.

The nights are the worst now; I can't escape facing it at night.

Sept. 14th: Julius had his birthday party at MacDonald's yesterday; it wasn't so bad. I've stopped taking sleeping tablets and I wish I had stopped sooner, I feel much better without them.

Oct. 3rd: I was thinking about things the other night and wondering why Clementine had to die. I was trying to make some sense out of it. I know she is not suffering — but I am. And what am I suffering from — losing her — not having her around for my sake? In fact I am suffering not for Clementine but for myself. I think that that is an indulgence on my part, and that one day I shall stop and get on with life again.

Nov. 27th: You won't believe this, Harris, yesterday I bought a bookshop in Chippendale. Frank had some assurance money which I didn't know about. Not much, but enough. There is a little house attached to the back of the shop which we will live in. I want you to see it, perhaps when I come and visit you.

Dec. 9th: I suppose I will never send this letter to you — it's more like therapy for me than anything else. Yesterday was the most enjoyable day I have spent since Clementine died. Thank you, Harris. We always did have nice times together, didn't we? Perhaps we are somewhat alike? I would like to think so.

The bookshop is a bit crowded, but I love it. I will be happy when Julius makes some friends.

This last bit is written tonight, since you have been under your house.
JULIUS AND I NEED YOU, SO COME OUT!

> LOVE,
> Helen.

Last week I got a letter via the cottage from Angela. It was pretty depressing, so Sam went to her place and told her mother that either Lewis went, or he would send copies of the letter to the Attorney-General's Department, and the *Mirror* newspaper. The newspaper was my idea.

Stephanie is still in hospital and doesn't look like she will come out for some time. Next week I think I'll drop in on Angela. Maybe we'll go and see Stephanie and take her those chocolates she wanted.

I thought about putting my address down in case you felt like dropping me a line or something when you heard all this. But knowing what we're all like you'd probably never get around to it, and even if you did, I'd probably never answer your letter anyway.

Helen said I could stay with her for a few weeks until I felt better. I don't think she knows how I feel about her. It's probably a bit ridiculous the way I sometimes imagine that we could be together — but I've found there are lots of ridiculous things in this world — impossible ones, unlikely ones, even outrageous ones. And do you know what; they are nearly always the best things.

I'll see ya.